ATTACK ON TITAN

THE HARSH MISTRESS OF THE CITY

PART 1

CREATED BY HAJIME ISAYAMA
A NOVEL BY RYO KAWAKAMI
ART BY RANGE MURATA

Attack on Titan
The Harsh Mistress of the City
Part 1

Created by Hajime Isayama
A Novel by Ryo Kawakami
Art by Range Murata

Translated by Jonathan Lloyd-Davies

VERTICAL.

Art by Range Murata.

Originally published in Japanese as *Shingeki no Kyojin: Kakuzetsu Toshi no Jouou 1*.

This is a work of fiction.

ISBN: 978-1-941220-62-7

Manufactured in the United States of America

First Edition

Vertical, Inc.
451 Park Avenue South
7th Floor
New York, NY 10016
www.vertical-inc.com

The Harsh Mistress
of
the City

CONTENTS

The Harsh Mistress of the City

of

the City

PROLOGUE

They were at breaking point. They all knew it.

The party of wagons thundered across the interior, throwing clouds of dust into the air. There were dozens in view. Their total number was even greater.

No…not the interior. It had *ceased to be the interior.*

It was the reason they were fleeing.

A group of Titans approached clumsily, their arms lumbering forwards. They were all stark naked. Outwardly human in form, they had heads that were either abnormally large or small, arms that were too long or short. Their eyes gave no hint of intelligence. They were a variety of sizes; even then, the shortest looked almost twice the height of a regular person. With nothing to which to stage a comparison, the plains made it impossible to scale their distance.

"Get cracking! Full speed ahead!"

"Do whatever it takes—buy them time! Keep those Titans back!"

The soldiers of the Garrison urged their horses on, vying desperately to safeguard the wagons. The Vertical Maneuvering

Attack on Titan

Equipment was all but useless in the open plains. Left with no means to permanently fell the Titans, the soldiers could do nothing more than buy time for the evacuees to break free.

Rita was astride one of the horses. The animals were valuable assets, each the equivalent of a life fortune. She was still a rookie, only in her second year of service, but she'd received special permission to command a steed.

In order to protect the citizens of Quinta District.

The wind was harsh, bitingly cold against her exposed ears. When her admission to the Garrison had been decided, she had chopped off her long blond hair. Due to this people often mistook her for a man—or more specifically, for a boy.

In view up ahead squatted a Titan with low-sloping shoulders. Plastered over its face was an expression of melancholy. This didn't mean the creature was in any way grieving. The Titans didn't harbor anything that resembled emotion.

The slope-shouldered Titan began to stretch an arm forwards. Beyond, a group of people scattered from an overturned wagon. With a broken leg, its horse thrashed like an insect in its death throes. The other wagons were giving the area a wide berth.

"Somebody?!"

Rita looked frantically around. None of her senior troopers were available to help. One was busy acting as a decoy, galloping fiercely away with three Titans in chase. Another had landed on a fallen Titan and was attempting to hack through the vital spot on the nape of its neck. As she watched, a Titan's fingers pinched the head of another of her fellow soldiers. Her ears picked up the man's screams. She looked away, suppressing a sudden urge to cry.

No one could aid her. If she was to save the defenseless evacuees, she needed to do it alone.

She heard a sound like thunder rip through the air. Friendlies, firing artillery from the top of the wall. Rita pulled sharply on the reins and made a beeline towards the overturned wagon.

You can make it...

She readied a blade in one hand.

The Titan's fingers were already closing on an evacuee who hadn't managed to get away. She was just a child, a little girl of about five, in simple clothes and with black hair bunched around the nape of her neck. No doubt terror-stricken, she had sunk onto the ground and was gazing up at the Titan, her small eyes stretched wide. For a split second, Rita hesitated.

Save the horse, or the girl?

"There's...nothing to even consider."

Steadying her aim, she fingered the trigger on the hilt of the blade. An anchor fired from the barrels slung around her waist, and they oscillated violently, held fast by her leather belt. Wire cut through the air and the anchor caught hold of the Titan's neck. Rita immediately readjusted the trigger, setting the wire to reel in. An incredible pressure exerted itself on the belt strapped around her body. She caught her breath as the world flickered dark.

The wire pulled her abruptly forwards. She gave in to the momentum. Her body began to rise, up and off the saddle where she sat. The wire spun into the cylinder on her back. The force of pressurized gas.

Rita was propelled rapidly up towards the Titan, to where the anchor had struck it. Her mount receded into the distance behind her.

The Titan cocked its head slightly and, still squatting, brought its half-outstretched arm back to pad around its neck. Rita twisted the hilt of her blade, pulling it at an angle to release the anchor from the Titan's flesh before its fingers found the wire. The action did not diminish her inertia.

She pirouetted in midair, simultaneously readying her blade. *Graze the Titan's flank, then slice through its neck.* That had been the plan, but it wasn't going to work; for whatever reason, the Titan had abruptly risen to its feet.

"That's what you do?!"

Rita crashed straight into the creature's belly. She flipped, started to tumble, and hit the ground with her shoulder. Spasming in even more pain, she let out a senseless wail and came dangerously close to dropping her blade. Somehow managing to pull herself onto all fours, she lifted her head.

The Titan was gazing down at her. On its face, the same

melancholic expression. It bent its torso forwards, blocking the sun, and reached down with both hands.

Fear. Dizziness. Her bladder threatening to release. Yet…

"I'm not done yet!"

Summoning all of her courage, Rita unsheathed her second blade. Brandishing one in each hand she swung them through the air, slicing through the Titan's fingers, which were each as thick as her arm. Fingertips the size of clubs rained down, all severed at the first knuckle. Unidentifiable plumes of steam began to gush from the remaining stumps. Rita could feel the stuffy heat on her skin.

Wearing the same melancholic look, the Titan withdrew its hand and gazed at its fingers, which were already regenerating at an abnormal pace. For the briefest moment, the Titan seemed to have forgotten about Rita and the evacuee.

"Run!" Rita shouted over her shoulder.

The girl showed no reaction. Her eyes were focused on a single point behind Rita. There lay the upturned wagon. Next to the horse, which was no longer moving, Rita could make out a couple of human forms, also unmoving. Perhaps the girl's parents. Rita gritted her teeth.

"Come with me!"

She turned her back on the Titan and sprinted towards the girl. Slipping her two blades into their sheaths, she scooped the girl up. The girl weighed more than expected. *I guess kids are heavy too,* Rita noted despite herself.

"Rita!"

The thuds of urgent hooves approached. When Rita looked she saw Wilco, one of the recruits from her year, racing up to them. His right hand wielded a blade and the reins of his steed; in his left he had the reins of the horse Rita had left behind. Though vigilant of the Titan, he came to a stop before her. The two horses shook their heads and wheeled their front legs in the air.

"Get on, quick!"

"Thanks."

Rita ran over, hauling the girl with her. Wilco brought his steed around then kicked off towards the Titan.

Rita boosted the girl onto her horse, keeping Wilco in her peripheral vision. He flanked the Titan and sliced right through the tendon behind its ankle. He briefly disappeared into the steam erupting from the wound. Rita pulled herself up and got into the saddle.

"Crap! How can they be so—it's hardly been a day! Not even a day since they breached Wall Maria!" raved Wilco inside the steam.

Another bombardment rang out, overpowering his voice. The air seemed to shudder.

"We messed up. We should've waited until night! Not now, in daylight, with Titans out! Evacuate, how?!"

News of the fall of Shiganshina—the district jutting from Wall Maria's southernmost point—had arrived the previous evening. It had resulted in an immediate decision to abandon Quinta, a district farther west along Wall Maria that Rita and the others called home. They were supposed to evacuate towards Wall Rose.

That had been just a few hours ago.

Positioning the girl in front to properly seat her, Rita craned to see the Titan.

If they're here already, they must have gotten through in no time at all...

The Titans had approached Quinta faster than expected. It suggested that they'd breached Shiganshina's gate to the interior within an hour of breaking into the district.

"It's coming!"

Wilco approached, slicing a path through the steam. Rita immediately tugged on the reins, driving her feet into her mount's flanks. It reared powerfully into motion. The girl was as stiff as an ornament in Rita's arms.

Rita stole a backwards glance. The steam was beginning to dissipate.

The Titan came abruptly into view. It was on all fours and reaching towards them. Fleeing its fingers Rita came up alongside Wilco.

They moved to rejoin the main force.

Attack on Titan

Mathias…

Rita bit back the name of her childhood friend. His image came to mind readily. A young man with a slightly broad forehead and gentle features, always looking vaguely troubled, he was the scion of a merchant association. His status had allowed him to leave Quinta at a relatively early juncture. Perhaps he'd made it to Wall Rose already; Rita wished from the bottom of her heart that he was safe.

A horrific scream pealed through the air.

Rita turned to see the soldier who had been leading the Titans away. He'd been caught by a seven-meter-class and was being devoured head first. The Titan had both hands clamped around the man's shoulders. The man's legs flailed, but in vain. There was a loud crunch as his skull splintered. His right leg began to convulse. After that, his entire frame went limp.

Another Titan approached, a five-meter-class. With the tips of its fingers, it plucked up her dead colleague's legs, slipped them into its mouth, and began to gnaw on them.

Rita's fellow soldier was being fed on by two Titans, working respectively from his head and his legs. Blood jetted from the neck. Blood sprayed from the knees. The two monsters continued to gorge, soaking their faces red with blood, moving closer until their noses touched.

"What the hell…" Wilco muttered.

Rita used one arm to pull her ward in tight and, with her

other hand, shielded the girl's eyes. That was when Rita noticed. She couldn't believe it.

"But that's…"

"Seriously?!"

Wilco must have seen the same thing. There, at the crest of a gradual incline beyond the caravan of wagons, emerged an even greater mass of Titans. The majority were three to five meters tall, but Rita noticed some that were almost three times as large.

"We can't keep this up. Don't let any more out!"

Following the booming voice, their commander pulled up on horseback. He appeared to mean the flow of evacuees from the gate. His blade was steaming. He had, it seemed, only just slain one of the Titans.

"You two return to the wall. Ensure the gate is closed!"

"Yes, sir!"

Rita and Wilco brought their steeds around and, side by side, began towards the gate. Rita glanced down at the girl seated against her belly.

It was probably for the best. With her to look after, Rita's ability to help was limited. And she wanted to deliver the girl through the wall and to safety as quickly as possible.

That very wall was pulling closer. It stood fifty meters tall, and at its foot, it was over ten meters thick. Its towering height had seemed endless, but now the wall looked awfully vulnerable, as though the Titans might scale it with ease.

Stunted wooden structures jostled on the near side. Until just hours earlier, large throngs of the poor had illegally settled there, in what had been the interior. Now the place was utterly devoid of people.

The poor had left for Wall Rose the moment word of Wall Maria's fall had arrived. Rita believed they had made the right decision since they had no hope of being allotted horses or wagons. As far as they were concerned, the only option was to cover as much distance as they could on foot before the Titans came.

As she'd feared, a group of Titans was already swarming around the shantytown. The cannons mounted on top of the wall targeted them and spat flame. There was a tumultuous roar and clouds of smoke distended into the air.

The girl in Rita's arms let out a muffled cry, and they felt the earth tremble through their steed. The wooden structures that had taken direct hits were decimated. Fragments seared into the air then rained back down. Angry shouts rose from the caravan of wagons. The bombardment had—unfortunately—failed to hit the Titans.

"Damned idiots!"

Rita raised her voice in response to Wilco's cursing. "We can't blame them. They're fresh recruits!"

The Training Corps had been assigned to man the cannons, all kids who had enlisted only a few weeks earlier. The soldiers of the Garrison Regiment had been sent into direct combat with the Titans.

Meanwhile, the Military Police Brigade—membership of which was open only to the highest-scoring graduates of the Training Corps—had departed for Wall Rose with the rest of Quinta's elite during the early stages of the evacuation. Rita's childhood friend Mathias would be under their protection.

Which means he'll be okay...

One of the shells slammed into a Titan nearing the foot of the wall.

"That's better!" Wilco yelled reflexively.

The Titan's wagon-sized head flew apart, spraying the air with bone, muscle, and something that resembled hair. The fragments stuck to the wall in gruesome, mottled patterns. Immediately they began to vent steam and to vanish whole. The headless Titan staggered and collapsed onto its rear end, pulverizing the wooden structure trapped underneath. Debris and steam shot up in dense clouds. By the time they cleared, the Titan's head was already in the process of regenerating.

"Insane... This is insane. Damn it!" Wilco spat the words along with spittle.

In front of Rita, the girl began to sob. No doubt her mind and emotions were starting to catch up with her.

Artillery crashed into the ground ahead. A huge blanket of dirt took flight, assaulting them in time with the blazing air. Rita's arm came up without thought, shielding the girl's face for a second time.

"We're going to…fall?!"

A gaping hole had been punched into the ground. Rita pulled her steed around, just barely managing to avoid the lip.

She navigated between burning houses. The fire was already spreading, and a Titan was slumped on its backside amidst the flames. A group of Rita's seniors in the Garrison were charging towards it.

Fierce battles unfolded in every direction. Her former class-mates and juniors, who had little field experience, were falling in quick succession. Yet, Rita forced herself to look away.

Not now!

They were to relay instructions to the soldiers beyond the wall to close the gate. It was not far now. From the gate a pas-sageway with a barrel-vaulted ceiling led inwards, five meters tall and three wide. Suspended on an array of chains above it were iron plates, reinforced with multiple layers, the same width as the passageway.

Wagons were being swallowed and spat out one after the other. Poorer citizens who hadn't been able to secure one were attempting to escape on foot. Some, who had come out only to witness Titans running amok, now crowded the entrance in a panic. Those who were still trying to leave the town clashed with the ones clamoring to go back in. They cursed and threw punch-es. Large numbers of men and women were bloodied and had broken noses, cuts on their eyes and mouths, and bruised fists, all without being attacked by the Titans themselves. The yells and indignant shouts were enough to make Rita's ears ache.

"Wh-What are you all doing? Hey!" Rita gave a hard flick of the reins. Her mount picked up speed. "Please, turn around. Go back! You'll be safer inside!"

"Get back. Hey, are you even listening? Do you want to die?" Wilco yelled, moving faster with Rita.

No one paid any notice. The line of wagons continued to push down the artery road. The count of Garrison soldiers protecting their passage was notably diminished. In contrast, the tally of gathering Titans was visibly greater.

"Shut the gate, this instant! Commander's orders!"

"Wilco, there are people..."

If they forced the gate closed now, people could get caught between the falling portal and the ground.

"We don't have the time. If they won't listen, we have to force them."

Rita supposed he had a point. "Yeah... Okay!"

"Damn it—they can't hear me!"

The cannons were still booming intermittently, and the air was filled with screams. There was absolutely nothing to suggest the gate was being closed.

"I'll tell the guys in charge, directly."

Wilco began to operate his Vertical Maneuvering Equipment.

He fired an anchor, embedding the tip in the ceiling near the passageway's entrance. He must have judged that he couldn't get through on horseback thanks to the evacuees jammed inside.

Just then a shell detonated in close proximity. A structure burst into flames, sending fragments of floor and wall and roof hurtling towards them. A slab of the debris hit the side of Wilco's head with a heavy thump.

His body immediately went limp. The Vertical Maneuvering Equipment was already pulling the wire in, but without accelerating any further. Moving like a string puppet, Wilco fell off his horse and hit the ground.

"Wilco?!"

The wire continued to reel in under the force of the compressed gas. Wilco's shoulders, rear end, and head were flung hard into the earth again and again. With each impact his limbs contorted unnaturally and blood sprayed from his skin. Rita desperately tried to catch hold of him, but he stayed ever so slightly out of reach.

The soldier continued to bounce and whirl, dragged along by the wire. He suddenly began to pick up speed; perhaps his finger was caught on the trigger on the hilt of his blade. The evacuees scrambled to get out of his way. His path was open.

The string puppet was now a tattered sack. Scattering blood, it lifted up from the ground. It climbed over the evacuees' heads, showering them.

The wire hit full recoil, crucifying Wilco where the anchor had dug in. There was a squelch like someone beating a wet cloth, followed by a crunch as his remaining bones shattered. Some poked visibly from his body. Even more blood spilled onto the evacuees who jostled below. This, at last, silenced them.

Around them, the bombardment continued to pound. Also faintly audible was the sound of the blazing fires, and the Titans' footfall and chomping.

Wilco was dead.

He'd died in vain.

No...I won't let it be in vain.

Rita clasped hold of the reins.

"Everybody, get back inside. We're closing the gate!"

Strange. The words flowed easily.

Strange. Her body was moving of its own accord.

She focused on a point straight ahead—Wilco's crucified form. Aiming a fraction to the left, she fired her anchor. The tip drove into the stone ceiling of the passageway. She felt the impact through the wire.

"Close your eyes."

Taking firm hold of the bawling girl, Rita rose up in her saddle. Depressing the trigger, she kicked into action the recoil of the wire. The equipment on her back growled and started to spin. An incredible force wrapped itself around her, and she and the girl were propelled into the air. Her arms felt ready to come off.

Attack on Titan

They sailed through the air. Wilco's crucified form rushed closer.

For a brief moment, Rita lost her composure. She came close to shrieking. But the girl's weight and heat—not warmth, it was heat she felt—allowed her to hold on to her senses.

Together, Rita and the young girl soared over the evacuees, who craned to watch when they caught sight of the pair.

Rita twisted the hilt of her blade again; setting the angle she pulled, freeing the hook from the ceiling. In an instant it wound fully in. Carried now by inertia, Rita and the girl continued to soar diagonally upwards. They would trace a trajectory then gently descend—or so she'd pictured it.

Instead Rita rammed shoulder-first into the curved ceiling, and pain shot from her head to her toes. The girl stiffened in her arms.

Rita came close to losing her grip. She gritted her teeth, endured it, and somehow channeled renewed strength into her arms to hold the girl tighter—tighter still.

"What the…?"

"Up there!"

They began to tumble towards the evacuees' heads. Rita considered firing an anchor before impact but didn't have the time. Instead, she noted the directions of the ceiling and the exit. Twisting around, she used her back and arms to protect the girl.

They scythed into a few of the evacuees. In a stroke of luck, they seemed not to have hit any children or seniors. The people around them cleared space amidst shrieks and jeers.

"Sorry…but I'm in a hurry!"

Rita adjusted her hold on the young girl and, without attempting to stand, fired an anchor at a section of the ceiling nearer the exit. She felt her belt constrict. She struggled for air. The next moment, she surfaced from the surrounding evacuees. One tried to grab her—probably a man she'd knocked over—but unable to match the pull of the Vertical Maneuvering Equipment, he cried out and pulled back.

Rita and the girl climbed diagonally up towards the ceiling once again. This time Rita was quicker to free the anchor but careened into the ceiling regardless. The impact was at least gentler. She rebounded and began to tumble diagonally, and again lacking the time to fire an anchor, she was flung towards the ground and another group of evacuees. Even as she was beginning to lose feeling in her arms, the pain ricocheting through her body refused to dissipate.

Repeating the process, Rita finally cleared the passageway. Her vision darkened, then light flooded back.

A vast crowd thronged inside the gate area, the majority carrying valuables or children on their backs. They were making frighteningly slow progress. Avoiding the densest clusters of people, Rita touched down. She let her limbs absorb the impact, then placed the girl gently down.

Attack on Titan

Rita raised her head and appealed to everyone around her.

"The Titans are close by! Leaving is too dangerous, go back to town for now."

She pressed the girl's diminutive frame into the arms of a middle-aged woman. The girl was utterly passive. No doubt she was finding it hard to process the events that had unfolded before her eyes. The middle-aged woman looked hesitant but accepted the girl.

Rita meant it when she told the girl, "Be strong, okay?"

Her parents were in all likelihood dead. If they had survived, they were continuing their evacuation on the other side of the wall. It was impossible to know when she'd see them again. The same applied to Rita and Mathias as far as that was concerned.

For now…the gate!

Forcing herself to change gears, Rita set off for a structure close to the gate and appended to the wall. She peered through the open doorway.

There.

As she'd expected, the post was manned by greenhorns from the Training Corps. They gazed at Rita with eyes on the verge of tears, their hands clasped around the crankshaft that opened and closed the iron gate. They knew they had to do something, but not what or how, and looked it.

Rita hollered, "Close it! Right now we have to shut the gate. Commander's orders. Hurry, before the Titans get through!"

"Hey, wait. What about us?"

"We won't be able to get away!"

"How is that fair?"

Voices of discontent rose from the civilians who had overheard. Rita turned and barked at them, "What's the point if we're all wiped out?!"

The trainees finally began to heave the enormous crankshaft around, releasing the chains. The gates began to come down in unison at either side of the passageway.

"Ouch. Reel them back!"

"Out of my... Stop it!"

Here and there shouts began to erupt after having once abated. No one cared to get sandwiched between the gates and the ground. There was a wild scramble to get out first, either beyond the wall or back into town.

But the gates didn't halt.

Little by little, the outside world was suppressed from view.

Wilco was first to go.

Flames lapped over the shanties. Rita's colleagues were embroiled in battle. Titans of varying sizes eyed the passageway with confusion. A few began to approach.

Mathias was out there, beyond it all.

The Harsh Mistress of the City

CHAPTER ONE

Mathias was dreaming. Reliving past experiences, aware that he was dreaming, but unable to wake regardless. A variety of scenes appeared then faded again. One eventually stuck, the outlines beginning to coalesce.

Needless to say, he recognized it right away.

It was the first time he'd met Rita.

Mathias was playing in a courtyard overflowing with green. Bright sunlight shone down. In the middle of the courtyard stood a fountain, a symbol of wealth. His father, Jörg, was chairman of the Kramer Merchant Association and one of the richest men in Quinta.

A man, still young, appeared in the hallway alongside the courtyard. Mathias felt his spirits lift. It was Henning, the district apothecary. He fashioned remedies for Mathias' mother and made regular visits to deliver them. She had been ill and confined to bed for the last few years. Although he usually came alone, this day was different.

A young girl stood by his side.

She looked around Mathias' age. Seven, perhaps eight. She

was clinging to the hem of Henning's garments, and she looked scared. At the same time she seemed entranced by the flamboyant build of the courtyard filled with greenery.

This had been their first meeting. At the time, Rita had worn her blond hair down below her shoulders.

Henning noticed Mathias and smiled and called out a greeting. He would have been around twenty-five at the time. Somehow he had the air of an artist about him.

Mathias returned the greeting: "Good day." He was following his father's teaching: *Members of the Kramer family must never forget their courtesy. Even with the laboring classes.*

"This is my daughter." Henning glanced warmly down at the girl to his side. "Your father was kind enough to suggest I bring her." The girl remained half-hidden behind her father, and he prodded her gently forwards. "Now, Rita, what do you say?"

The girl opened her mouth but couldn't manage any words. Her face grew increasingly flushed until, finally, her eyes fell to the ground and she again sought refuge behind her father's back.

"A little shy, this one. Think you could be friends?"

"Yes, of course," Mathias supplied another perfect answer. He turned to face the girl—to face Rita. "My name is Mathias. It's nice to meet you."

"H…H…Hello," the girl just about managed a response.

Very well done, thought the young Mathias. He'd heard that some of the laboring classes lacked even the concept of greetings.

He couldn't say the girl was gracious, not by any standard, but she was at least making an attempt to be friendly.

A couple of seconds later the girl added, "Ri…ta," a little flustered.

It took Mathias a moment to recall that this was in fact her name. Perhaps she'd realized that, as he'd introduced himself, she needed to as well. He felt more and more taken by the girl.

"I should see your father first," Henning said, lifting his eyes to the second floor. "Then it's your mother's checkup. Would you mind keeping Rita company for a while?" Henning's eyes flicked back to his daughter.

"Of course. I can give her the tour."

It was a phrase his father often used: *Let me give you the tour.*

Henning's smile broadened. "Impressive, very becoming of the heir to a merchant association. Rita, make sure to pay attention to what Mathias shows you."

The girl looked apprehensive but gave her father a sharp nod regardless.

At that point the outline of the world began to lose cohesion. Mathias found himself coming close to calling out Rita's name.

The remembered scene receded, to be replaced by another.

As before, they were in the courtyard of the Kramer mansion.

Mathias and Rita were mostly unchanged, but there had been a shift in mood between them. Rita had already made a number of visits. While still a little deferential, she had become for the most part able to converse without hesitation.

"It's this way, in the corner."

Mathias crossed to the edge of the courtyard, but only after a careful scan of the surrounding cloisters. An afternoon sun inundated them. Apart from the two of them the mansion was empty—Mathias' father and his retinue of servants were away.

Mathias crouched next to the roots of a tree and used his hand to clear some of the dirt. As he did, a metal handle came into view.

"Watch this."

He hooked his fingers around it. With both feet planted firmly in the ground, he tipped his weight backwards. A square line appeared, rising slowly as an iron cover. The dirt and sand piled on top just trickled away. Rita stared in blank amazement.

"Mathias, what—"

"Just a second. I have to be careful, so it doesn't fall."

Keeping hold of the handle Mathias circled around and rotated the cover a half-circle before letting it gently down on the far side. Where the cover had been was a gaping hole a meter long and wide. A brick staircase led downwards.

"Come on then. There's treasure I want to show you."

"But…are we allowed? Without permission?"

"No, not really. I suppose Father would be mad if he found out. He doesn't know that I know."

"Well, maybe we shouldn't…" Rita fidgeted with her hands and looked warily around.

"I'll deal with him if he finds out. I'm pretty sure he'll let it go if I say sorry. I can tell him I found it by chance and went in because I was curious. Come on." Mathias lowered a foot down onto the first step and held a hand out towards Rita. "It's a little dark, but it's not scary if we leave the cover open."

"Okay." Rita, still hesitant, held out her hand. Their fingers made contact.

For some reason Mathias' heart was beating hard.

Even though he'd explored the basement room any number of times before. Even though he knew there was no reason to be nervous.

Then he realized: It was the first time he and Rita were holding hands. Maybe that was why he was getting so worked up. He *had* heard that men became excited when they touched women.

Rita was still peering nervously around, apparently of two minds, but there were flashes of anticipation, of excitement, in her eyes. It seemed unlikely, however, that being in contact with Mathias was the cause.

Together, they carefully treaded down the stairs. Rita's hand felt amazingly warm. It was trembling a little and had a faint sheen of sweat.

The layout inside was nothing complicated. The stairs led down to a single underground room about five meters on each side. An adult might have found the ceiling a little low, but it was nothing to concern Mathias and Rita at the time. A collection of holes where the walls joined the ceiling filtered light into the room. Mathias knew they were positioned to lie in the shadows of various columns and the fountain.

Their eyes quickly adjusted to the penumbra.

"W-Wow!" Rita gasped.

Arranged neatly against the walls were objects of all sizes: sculptures and pots, shields, suits of armor that bore intricate motifs. An almost complete lack of dust attested that they were all well looked after.

"Father's treasures. He keeps a few in his study, upstairs, but there are more here."

"I-I've never seen anything like it."

"They're called *artworks*, apparently. Worth a king's ransom."

"A king's ransom!"

"I think that's why he keeps them hidden. People might frown if they thought he had too many."

It was something Mathias' father Jörg often repeated. That members of merchant associations and the royal government belonged to the privileged class. That the privileged were able to live extravagant lifestyles. In exchange, they were duty-bound to serve the laboring classes, to devote themselves to society as a whole rather than to personal gain.

However, they were not to flaunt their lifestyles without

reason. There were people who didn't understand the interplay of authority and duty, and it would not do to agitate them unnecessarily. Of course, even they were to be served. At the time Mathias had yet to develop a full understanding of such ideas. Even so, he had an intuitive grasp of why it was important not to "flaunt their lifestyles."

"It's why he prefers to savor them in secret, by himself."

"Savor?" Rita walked up to a naked sculpture of a man. She moved her head in to study the detail, but seemed to lack the courage to actually touch it.

"To see and enjoy. *To savor such things is to refine one's soul.* That's what Father always says."

"How? You can refine your soul?"

"I'm not really sure, but he says it does wonders for his state of mind. If that's true, though, I think Father should display them for more people to see."

"I want to show my dad, too."

"You can't. Remember, this place is secret."

Rita gave him a sincere nod in response and replied, "Sure." She sucked in a deep breath, as though she was trying to absorb as much of the sculpture's refined air as she could.

Watching this Mathias said, "We can come here again."

"Really?!" Rita spun around, joy on her face.

"Really. On the condition that you tell no one."

"Right. Okay." Rita nodded feverishly. "Promise?"

"I promise."

Her features were lit under a thin column of light. She seemed to be having trouble believing her luck.

Then, the pictures from Mathias' memory began again to transition.

They were no longer children. Neither were they full-grown adults.

Mathias sat at the dining table with Rita's family. It was their living quarters on the second floor above Henning's apothecary. Wooden floorboards and white, stuccoed walls. There was no comparing them to the Kramer's dining chambers, and the whole space was probably smaller than the mansion's kitchen. Nonetheless, Mathias had kept up regular visits even after he was in his teens. He saw no harm in routinely exposing himself to the lifestyle and ideas of the laboring classes. It would help him think up—or search out—goods that pleased them. As Jörg had told him: *Always consider the popular opinion.*

Such motivations aside, Mathias quite enjoyed spending time with Rita's family. On the table were candles and a paraffin lamp whose warm light perfectly complemented the room's atmosphere.

"We're so sorry to call on you like this," Rita's mother, Doris, said as she dished out their food.

She was an energetic and spirited woman. This contrasted

with her husband's more gentle disposition, but Mathias had never once seen them argue.

Mathias had lost his mother to sickness just two years earlier. As a result he was envious of the relationship shared by Rita, Henning, and Doris, but he never felt true envy. Even with his mother alive and well, he would not be enjoying the sort of ties Rita did with her family. Mathias' relationship to his parents was more formal, and he didn't view this as necessarily bad. It was simply the way of privileged families.

"Not at all—I was glad for the invitation. It's a perfect break. The truth is my father had expressed a wish to come too. Unfortunately he finds it a little more difficult to slip away."

"Out of the question! We couldn't possibly host anyone as august as the chairman of the Kramer Merchant Association," the mother shooed, and the daughter chimed in, "Yeah, I mean, he makes regular trips to the capital, doesn't he?"

Mathias shook his head. "He's nothing special. He does like to keep busy, of course."

Since the loss of his wife, Mathias' father Jörg had thrown himself into his work with even greater ferocity.

Henning decanted wine into everyone's glasses. Today they were celebrating a special occasion.

"As I'm sure will you, Mathias," he said. "One day soon you'll find yourself no less busy."

"Exactly—this could well be the last time you visit us here."

"Yeah, I bet." A look resembling that of an abandoned puppy flashed over Rita's face.

What they were saying was probably true. The merchant association was busy, and the volume of work was only expected to increase.

Mathias forced himself to sound relaxed when he responded, "There's no need to exaggerate. I'll be barging in every now and then if only you'll let me."

"Well, you're always welcome, Mathias."

It was clear that Doris was being genuine. She welcomed him not as the scion of a merchant association, but independently of his status, and never sought anything in return. Rita and Henning were the same.

It was comforting, and Mathias felt grateful. By then he was already beginning to receive preferential treatment from those around him. The stream of people who approached with ulterior motives was never-ending.

"All that aside, the amazing one here is Rita," Mathias changed the subject to the young woman next to him. She was dressed in the uniform of the Garrison Regiment. It was brand-new and crisply starched, without a single crease or blemish.

"Hmm? Me?" Rita blinked in apparent surprise.

Mathias nodded. "Joining the Training Corps, getting all the way to the end."

Many citizens entered the Training Corps by the time of their fifteenth birthday. This didn't mean they all became soldiers. A certain percentage was guaranteed to flunk out.

Rita, however, had lasted her two-year training period to become an official member of the Garrison Regiment. While she may not have ascended to the Military Police Brigade—entry to which was restricted to an elite group of the highest achievers—Mathias had heard that she had excelled among her classmates.

"I know, such a surprise! Who'd have known she had that kind of backbone? Though you'd be shocked how strong her arms—"

"Mom, that's terrible!"

"You'd never have imagined it, going by how she used to be." Henning regarded his daughter with a dazzled grin. "She never even went out and preferred to be cooped up indoors."

"And look at her now, a soldier."

"Yes, well…" Rita drooped her head, peering up at Mathias. "That's thanks to Mathias."

"Indeed. You're spot on there," Doris agreed with a deep nod. "Didn't get on with the neighborhood kids at all. If Mathias here hadn't kindly offered a hand, well, who's to know how you'd have ended up!"

"You have our thanks," Henning said, lifting his glass and tipping his head towards Mathias. Following his signal, the others reached for their own drinks.

"Please, there's no need. I was just the same as Rita. I didn't even go to school." During his childhood, Mathias had been taught exclusively by his personal tutor, one of the mansion's servants. "I didn't have any friends my own age. Rita was irreplaceable in helping me learn about the outside world."

"That's silly. Definitely not true." Rita cast her eyes downward, her face flushed as though drunk.

But Mathias' gratitude to her was genuine.

"Now, shall we make a toast?" Doris suggested.

"To celebrate the end of Rita's training and her joining the Garrison."

Following Henning's prompt, they all cried, "Cheers!"

"Make sure you eat your fill," Doris urged. "Today's a treat. I mean, it probably won't compare to what our betters are… Ah, mmm, that's by the by. Sorry if I'm being annoying."

"Not at all." Mathias smiled and began to help himself to the oil-pickled fish, stewed meats, steamed vegetables, and variety of cheeses on display across the dining table. "This is really great."

"A-ha, flattery!"

"I mean it."

"Thank you. I'm glad, even if you're just being polite." Doris showed a big smile. Adding food to all of their plates, she said, "You know you really have grown into such a decent young man. Never once rebelling."

"It's true," Henning agreed, "you find so many *prodigal sons* out there."

"They're just a minority."

"Maybe, but I believe you're studying hard in preparation to inherit your father's position?"

"Well, yes. But I enjoy it."

Every day, Mathias' father Jörg drilled into him all kinds of knowledge, from stock fulfillment, sales strategies, and managerial techniques to methods of ingratiating oneself with the royal government. It wasn't an easy life, but it was worthwhile. And Mathias believed it when Jörg told him that hardship builds character.

"Well, I think it's admirable. In light of our situation," Doris turned her eyes to her daughter.

Rita shrank into her chair. "You're making my ears sting."

"When this one was little, she was always calling 'Daddy' and trying hard to learn the ropes."

"Medicine?"

"That's right. Then before we know it she finds this obsession with being athletic. I do wonder if it was in her blood."

"Huh? My blood?"

"Oh, nothing. Umm…you know…just that I used to be partial to a bit of exercise, too, when I was younger." The answer sounded evasive especially since this was Doris.

"You did? I didn't know that about you, Mom."

"Anyhow," Henning intervened, "Rita doesn't need to worry about the business." No doubt thinking about the apothecary below, he threw an unconscious glance toward the stairs. "I'd be happy to end it at my generation. It's nothing special."

"Yes, I suppose so," Doris seconded with a big nod.

"You don't need to do that! I'm not going to let it fold. I'm planning to take it over someday, and I still study remedies... sometimes?"

"Don't look at me," Mathias recused himself with a wry smile.

Their dinner to celebrate Rita's entry into the Garrison proceeded without further mishap. Eventually it grew late, and they brought it to a close.

"I'll walk with you back to the mansion," Rita offered as Mathias got to his feet.

"No, it's okay. You'd be alone for the return trip. That's far more dangerous."

"I'll be fine, I've got my training. What do you think I joined the Garrison for?"

"Yes, it *is* what she does now!" "A first duty to commemorate!" her parents chimed in.

"Well, if you insist..."

Losing three against one, Mathias left the house with Rita.

Together they wended through the nighttime town's alleys.

The sky blinked with stars. The streets were cast in pale light from the nearby houses. It was busier than they'd expected, and they passed people scurrying home, late-shift workers on their way out, jovial drunks.

"It really is great news. Congratulations," Mathias said, still faced forwards.

"Thanks."

"I'd have probably been against it if you'd said it was the Survey Corps. But I'm honestly glad to hear you joined the Garrison."

The former was tasked to investigate the world outside the walls. As they were all but guaranteed to encounter and battle with Titans, more than twenty percent of their number ended up losing their lives with each operation.

"My parents said the same. That they'd have been against my joining the Survey Corps."

"The Garrison also performs bodyguard duty, doesn't it? For example, escorting merchant association members when they travel to other towns."

"That's right."

Journeying to another town did not mean leaving the walls to brave the lands where the Titans roamed. It only necessitated crossing through the interior. An escort detail merely needed to watch out for bandits or feral dogs.

Mathias went on. "So there's a chance we could travel together. South to Shiganshina, or into the interior and Fuerth."

"That…would be great. I'll make sure to do my best."

"Do your best?"

"They're more open to requests if you've performed well."

"Ah, I see."

"Yeah."

Rita let her hand brush over the hilt of the blade slung around her waist. The sheath contained the firing control for the Vertical Maneuvering Equipment; on her back she wore the motor that recoiled the wire. Mathias couldn't say it really suited her. Maybe he just needed to grow used to seeing her with it on.

"The truth is, I wanted to join too."

"Join? The Corps?"

"Right. The Training Corps." Before he realized, Mathias had begun his confession. He wasn't even sure why he'd chosen to broach the topic.

"You did?"

"I actually told Father I wanted to join, one time. It didn't work. He just told me: 'Everyone has a duty to fulfill. Yours is to devote yourself to people as part of the merchant association.'" Mathias had spent a long period in deliberation but had eventually taken his father's words on board.

"Wow. I had no idea."

"That would be because I never told you."

They crossed a stone bridge. There was the faint susurration of water. Moonlight sparkled, reflecting off the surface.

Mathias continued to talk, his mouth seeming to work independently of his will. "I sometimes wonder why it has to be me.

I think to myself that anyone could perform the same duty, and just as well. That all I have going for me is that I happened to be born a Kramer."

"That's just—"

"Which is why," Mathias cut in, "I wanted to believe I had at least the same abilities as everyone else. To prove I was skilled enough to be a soldier if I'd wanted. Then I'd be *choosing* to serve in the merchant association."

"That's why you wanted to join the Corps?"

"Yes."

"Nonsense." Rita gave a reprimanding shake of her head. "You work really hard. You say you just happened to be born a Kramer, and yes, perhaps that's true, but I'm sure people who weren't born into it mostly don't show your level of determination."

Taken aback by this, Mathias found himself gazing intently into Rita's face. She wasn't particularly taciturn, but she certainly wasn't the type to wax eloquent.

Nevertheless, it was with increasing fire that Rita continued, "There are so many jobs in the world, it's impossible to experience them all. So there's no way to really know who's best suited to a particular role. In other words…I'm not sure how to say this, but all we can do is choose the work we'd be best at from among whatever options we have."

Mathias was stunned. Until then he'd always considered Rita

his junior, psychologically. He'd styled himself a kind of guardian who watched out for her. Perhaps the opposite had been true.

She was peering at him now with a worried look on her face. "You don't want to? Work for the merchant association."

"No, that's not it. It's not that I dislike the work… Actually, I quite enjoy it. I'm always learning something new."

"Then you should do it with confidence in yourself."

"Yes, you're right." Then, suddenly wondering, Mathias asked, "How about you? What made you want to become a soldier?"

"That…" replied Rita, turning ahead, her voice muted, "That's a secret."

Mathias traced back to their earlier conversation.

Working for the Garrison included bodyguard duty.

They might be able to travel to another town together.

Requests were heeded if a soldier performed well…

That couldn't be why she'd wanted to join the military, could it? Because she wanted to work alongside him? If that was it… didn't that mean she liked him?

Mathias, himself, had feelings for her. As far back as he could remember, he had no other friends his own age. She had broadened his horizons, and he'd said as much during their dinner.

He stole another look at her profile.

She didn't have the refined looks of girls from the privileged classes. But there was a definite beauty in her fresh vitality. More than anyone else Mathias knew, she was stridently individual and amazingly strong. She was furnished with an unshakable sense of right and wrong. If he asked her to become more than friends, she might say yes. While it was hard to imagine, he supposed they might start to go out together.

But what would happen then?

They might be happy for a number of years, but Mathias didn't think that his father, Jörg Kramer, would ever consent to their marriage. Mathias was destined to become the head of his household. He was expected to establish matrimonial ties with a family who had influence in the royal government or who represented one of the other merchant associations. Such marriages of convenience were a part of work, one of the duties his social status demanded of him.

But it was stupid to worry about such things at this stage. He was no doubt just getting ahead of himself. He wasn't even sure Rita had similar feelings for him. He felt ashamed for having let such wild fancy suck him in so quickly.

That had been just over a year ago.

Mathias sprang up.

For a moment he was thrown by the unfamiliar ceiling. Then he remembered. He was no longer at the family mansion in Quinta District. The warm comfort of the courtyard was gone. Mathias and the others had traveled into the interior the whole of last night, reaching Fuerth District on the western flank of Wall Rose. The room he was in now was a guest room in his father's townhouse. He'd stayed here a number of times before while accompanying the senior Kramer on business.

Weak afternoon light streamed through the window. The sun was already getting ready to set. He'd apparently been asleep for quite some time. He got down from the bed and slipped on his shoes.

It was cold. He hurried over to the closet, took out a jacket, and slipped it on. His luggage was unpacked and sorted. One of the servants must have seen to it while he was asleep. His memory seemed finally to clear.

Of course. He'd been so exhausted when they'd arrived in the morning, he'd collapsed into the bed and fallen fast asleep.

He stepped through the door. The wood-floored hallway showed no sign of life, but he sensed the presence of people downstairs.

"Father!"

Mathias half-tumbled down the steps. He stopped on a landing when he noticed Suzanne, one of their servants and his home tutor, talking with someone in the entranceway. Perhaps she was detailing to a worker whatever items they needed sent across.

She had been in the employ of the Kramer family for as long as Mathias could remember and had to be in her late thirties. She looked a good ten years younger, though, and they were more like friends than teacher and student.

"Do you know about the others? Everyone from Quinta. Have they made it already?" Mathias asked as he reached the first floor. He had in mind Rita, Henning, and Doris.

"Oh, Mathias…"

A faint look of pain flickered onto her face. Mathias didn't fail to pick up on the change. He couldn't have missed it, even if he'd wanted to.

"Did something happen?" He took a step closer. "What about Rita, her family? Are they here?"

"Not yet." Suzanne's answer was unambiguous, even as she hesitated, averting her eyes.

"Why?"

"The Titans—they arrived earlier than expected. That's what I was told. So…half of the population got stranded inside."

"Does that…" …*mean Rita is there too?*

Suzanne didn't answer. She wouldn't look up.

Why? "What—what happened?"

"The Garrison Regiment was deployed, to protect the evacuees." Her voice was trembling, her mouth quivering as she spoke. "They told me that, apart from a few, they were all wiped out."

It dawned on Mathias what she was trying to say.

Rita was dead.

At the very least, nobody knew if she had survived. Mathias felt as though a chasm had opened inside him.

"Why not?!"

Mathias was openly arguing with his father. It was perhaps the first time he'd ever done so. Jörg's work colleagues had gathered in the townhouse's study and stood around the large writing desk. Mathias recognized a few of the faces, but there were some he'd never seen before. The latter had to be representatives of the Fuerth merchant associations or delegates from the royal government.

"This matter concerns the survival of a great many people. And it isn't something I'm able to influence by myself."

"That's not true! Of course it's within your influence. You have the resources to mobilize soldiers whenever you see fit. Isn't it the merchant associations that keep the military stocked with food and equipment?"

"Yes, but these are not normal circumstances. You must understand at least that much."

"They might get through the wall if we don't act now!"

After hearing about Quinta from Suzanne, Mathias had requested Jörg to dispatch a rescue party. *Negotiate with the government through the merchant association!* But convincing Jörg had proven difficult.

"We know they managed to close the gate siding the interior. The Titans might have breached Wall Maria, but that doesn't mean Quinta is about to fall too."

"They're completely isolated. They'll run out of food." The district had been hemmed in by Titans on both its interior and exterior sides. The terror its residents had to be facing was unfathomable.

"They have stockpiles."

"They'll run out, eventually."

"I'm not saying that I intend to do nothing. Our guests are here to discuss potential measures." Jörg motioned his eyes toward his assembled colleagues. The large writing desk did have sheets of paper strewn roughly across its surface. Mathias didn't doubt that they had been in the middle of a heated debate when he'd come running in.

"What kind of measures?" he asked.

Jörg remained utterly impassive. "It's of no concern to you."

"Why not? You always bring me in for your meetings, whatever they are about. You tell me to watch closely and to pay attention. You say experience is everything."

"We lack the time to be dealing with amateurs. As I just told you, these arc not normal circumstances."

"But—"

"You've lost your composure. People who fail to remain calm are a liability. Even as I speak you impede the progress of our talks."

Jörg's colleagues neither agreed nor disagreed. They simply exchanged a few uncomfortable glances. Mathias knew he couldn't challenge his father's words, but he was far from satisfied.

"Mathias, I will do my best. You must understand."

Jörg, who was aware how close his son was to Rita, how they'd been friends since childhood, stared straight into Mathias' eyes. It went without saying that the senior Kramer recognized Mathias' worries and his desire to confirm as quickly as possible that Rita was safe. That was exactly why he was asking that Mathias "understand."

There was nothing Mathias could say to alter his father's stance. He realized that much at least.

"Of course… Gentlemen, please forgive me barging in."

He bowed his head to the assembled dignitaries then turned on his heels.

Mathias fled the townhouse. He feared he might go mad if he sat idle.

He roamed the streets with no clear purpose in mind. The ground was cobbled stone, with white stuccoed buildings rising to either side.

The appearance of the town was unchanged since his previous visit. The atmosphere, however, was notably different. The air was charged and tense. Passersby wore tight expressions and nobody smiled. Until now, Fuerth had been located wholly within the interior. Great walls and vast tracts of land had locked it away from the Titans' domain. But the status quo had undergone a dramatic shift.

It was exactly as Jörg had said. The monsters were converging towards the district's own wall. For the residents of Fuerth, the events in Shiganshina were very much their business.

"The wall…"

Before Mathias knew, he had arrived at it—on the side facing Wall Maria, which surely now had to be labeled the exterior.

Fifty meters tall, mankind's lifeline.

Right now the setting sun cast it in dark shadow. Below, where it met with the ground, were rows of basic lodgings that had been thrown up by the refugees.

"But we've only been here half a day…"

The majority of the structures consisted of nothing but cloth strung over supports scavenged from disassembled wagons. They were little more than tents. At the same time, a few buildings were made from wood and other more substantial materials. Huddled between them, refugees were busy beginning preparations for their evening meals, lighting stoves and setting pots and pans. The smell of the cooking wafted over, faintly mixed with the odor of sweat and human waste. Mathias was forced to realize that not everyone had townhouses to sleep in like he did.

"What am I doing?"

Members of the privileged classes were duty-bound to serve the masses, obligated to help. And yet Mathias was, at present, unable to do a thing. The majority of evacuees were being forced to live in discomfort, and Rita…hadn't even managed to escape. There was even the possibility that she'd given her life in an attempt to protect everyone else.

No. Wrong.

She was in Quinta, and she was alive. Waiting even now for assistance.

"Yes. She has to be…"

Mathias noticed something: a line of people in the periphery of his vision. Perhaps they were rationing food provisions. For some reason, the majority of those lining up were young men.

He began to walk towards the front of the line. The men threw him suspicious looks. He felt a little tense; the laboring classes were known for being short-tempered. And he'd heard that many nurtured an ill-founded dislike of the privileged classes—that they held the privileged responsible for everything lacking in their own lives. Even though, Mathias knew, the truth was the other way around. The privileged classes' able efforts supported the people, who would have no choice but to live like animals if not for the elites' intellect and knowledge.

But no, the people couldn't see it. Fixated on mere outward differences in lifestyle, they seized on every chance they could to voice condemnation.

Mathias wasn't dressed in a way that made him stand out. Just a cotton shirt with woolen trousers and a jacket, a common and unassuming outfit. Yet even now he remained conspicuous among the other young men who stood in line. There was the cleanliness of his skin and hair, the quality of fabric he wore. He didn't doubt that he offered a striking contrast.

Looking around he couldn't see anyone from social strata comparable to his own. He became acutely aware of the innumerable eyes trained on him. Redoubling his efforts to pay no attention, he focused instead on reaching the front of the line. He came to an unexpected halt when he saw the building up ahead.

"The barracks?"

The stone edifice towered upwards in line with the wall. The grounds stretching out behind it seemed to be of considerable size. The crest of the Garrison Regiment—twin roses over a shield—hung beside the main entrance.

The line came to an end just in front of the building. A desk had been set up in the middle of the street. Uniformed troops sat interviewing the refugees at the front of the line, scribbled notes, then handed separate slips of paper to the young men before sending them on their way.

"Don't even think about cutting in."

Startled by the harsh voice, Mathias spun around. "You mean me?"

"Who else?"

The voice belonged to a hawk-eyed youth with noticeably

bulging arms. The archetypal image of the laboring classes. The type of person it was best not to needlessly aggravate. Mathias was unhappy to note that his own hands were trembling slightly. Why was he letting himself get so intimidated by people like these?

Making sure to appear polite but firm, Mathias countered, "I'm not about to cut in. And I won't, but what are you all queued up for? I assume this isn't for food provisions?"

The youth exchanged glances with the men lined up around him. "Yeah right, we should be so lucky."

"They're recruiting volunteer soldiers. Don't bother if you ain't got the backbone," a squat man with broad shoulders added from behind. He looked a little older.

"Volunteer soldiers?"

"We're gonna take Shiganshina back," the hawk-eyed youth explained. "If we jam the hole, that'll stop any more Titans getting in. After that we only need to take down the ones between Wall Rose and Wall Maria, and all's back to normal."

It was true that success was far more likely if they were mopping up a limited number of Titans rather than battling a never-ending flow.

"The plan is to send in a vanguard and see."

"Only just been announced. Not surprising you hadn't heard yet."

"Wait, you said the plan is to take back Shiganshina? What

about Quinta?"

How could they be planning to leave Quinta alone when Rita and so many other people were stranded inside? Although the young man in front of him had done nothing wrong, Mathias had ended up sounding accusatory.

The hawk-eyed youth shrugged. "Quinta's safe. Well, maybe not *safe*. But the Titans haven't got in at least."

"I'm worried too. My wife and kids are back there," the middle-aged man with the broad shoulders added. "But the government's telling us our first priority is to take care of the Titans. Who are we to say otherwise?"

"I'm sure we'll check it out at least," cut in a plump man, who looked anywhere between twenty and forty. "Whole load of villages between Wall Rose and Wall Maria. Might be there's people there who didn't make it all the way."

"Meaning, we do what we can, but our main goal is to take back Shiganshina," the hawk-eyed youth said in conclusion.

Inasmuch as the plan placed Quinta on the back burner, the thinking matched Jörg's…or rather, it was probable that Mathias' father had played an important part in drafting the plan.

Of course. How could he not be involved? It seemed very likely that the operation was exactly what they'd been discussing in the study. If nothing else, they would have debated which supplies would be provided by which associations and to which theater. And yet his father had chosen to keep Mathias in the dark.

"Unbelievable…" He was being treated like a child, taken out of the loop on key matters.

"You one of the refugees?" the man with the broad shoulders asked.

"Yes. Sort of."

"Like I said, don't bother if you ain't got the backbone."

"Dressed like that, I don't imagine you need it," the hawk-eyed youth said, sneering a little. It was safe to assume he wasn't particularly well disposed to the privileged classes.

"Need it?"

"Money. Compensation."

"I see. If you volunteer, you receive compensation…"

It was obvious now that he considered it. Part of the money would be donated from the fortune of the Kramer Merchant Association. Mathias cast a fresh look down the line. The back seemed to stretch even farther.

"And that's why you're all…"

"That's true for some, but you'll find all kinds here. Myself? I'm not in it for the money," the man with the broad shoulders asserted.

Mathias remembered what the man had said earlier. "Of course, your wife and children."

"I was sure they'd come on ahead, you know. Then I hear they hadn't been able to find a wagon. So I've no choice, gotta clear the Titans if I'm to see them again."

"Seems there's people from Fuerth here too, the poor. In no small number," the plump man added in his shrill voice.

"I can see the attraction. You're guaranteed some money, and if you slay a Titan you become a hero."

"Damned fools, the lot of them." The man with the broad shoulders stared ahead, eyes brooding. "They ain't seen it. Only reason they can talk like that."

"Do you mean you did see? A Titan, attacking somebody?"

"Didn't just see it—I'd be dead if I'd been two wagons back."

"Wow…"

Mathias' thoughts jumped to Rita. *Right.* There was a chance this man knew if she was safe or not.

"What about soldiers? Garrison soldiers. Were they there with you?"

"They were. Why do you ask?"

"How were they…doing?" Mathias tripped over the words.

The man looked puzzled, but narrowed his eyes as though tracing his memory. "They were doing all they could. Fighting hard to protect us. I was watching through a gap in the tarp, mind, so I can't say for sure. Even then…" He faltered there.

"What?"

"I heard that most of 'em died. Can't say I'm surprised. It was hell out there."

The Titans were said to devour their victims indiscriminately. This man had no doubt witnessed such a sight firsthand. An image briefly formed in Mathias' mind of Rita writhing in agony, but he quickly pushed it away and asked the man another question. "How about a young female soldier with blond…short blond hair. Did you see anyone like that?"

"I don't think so. Mind you, would've been the last thing on my mind. I think that was true of all of us."

The three men regarded Mathias with what were now grave looks. They had doubtless guessed his predicament.

The plump man opened his mouth. "The soldier, she a friend?"

"Yes. A friend."

"There's a lot here like you," said the broad-shouldered man. "People who've had a lover or family killed, volunteering with a mind for revenge."

"Doesn't mean they're better than us. I'm volunteering to support myself, so I don't have to beg in the streets," the hawk-eyed youth muttered irritably.

The man with the broad shoulders nodded. "You're free to do as you like."

"But," Mathias, a thought suddenly occurring to him, inquired of the broad-shouldered man, "how can you do this—after having survived such a traumatic experience?"

"I see it the other way around." He brought his muscular shoulders up in a shrug. He had probably held a job in manual labor. "It's because I did that I know I've got to fight, to make sure my family never has to go through what I did."

After that, Mathias thanked the three men, then added himself to the back of the line. It went without saying that he had decided to volunteer for the operation to reclaim Shiganshina. As part of the campaign, he could travel outside the wall. That meant he might be able to reach Quinta. Unlike the man with the broad shoulders, Mathias wasn't interested in taking the fight to the Titans first. His most pressing need was to ensure Rita's wellbeing. He hoped, if possible, to bring her back to Fuerth where things were—at least for now—safe.

The sun grew lower, spreading longer and longer shadows. The volunteers and buildings were slowly fading into uniform darkness even as Mathias stared at them.

He suddenly came back to his senses.

Did he really need to go this far? It was true that he treasured Rita as a friend. She was the one person in the world whom he could wholly trust. The one person who accepted him for who he was. He felt secure with her.

In other words, he was in love.

The unshakeable truth revealed itself for the first time at precisely that moment.

Yet some cool-headed part of him began to blare out words of warning: *So what? Are you going to let some fleeting emotion get the better of you? Let it go. Live in accordance with your status.*

However he looked at it, his second thoughts were on the

mark. Even if Rita felt the same, they could never end up to-gether. Even if he brought her back from Quinta, after facing the greatest of dangers his only gain would be "to have saved a close friend," a mere trifle. Wasn't it better to remain in Fuerth, to sub-mit to his father, to learn the business at his side and to prepare for the future? He was the heir to the Kramer estate, the future head of the family. To put himself in physical danger, and all for the sake of one girl—there was no behavior more self-centered, so completely unrelated to serving the people.

And yet... Mathias couldn't bring himself to walk away from the line. If anything he was getting fed up with its slow progress.

Rita's image refused to leave his mind. He was beside himself with worry that she was badly injured or suffering from hunger. Mathias would get to Quinta by hook or by crook. The feeling came like a premonition. It was as though a stranger were deter-mining his actions, his decisions.

Perhaps I'm not qualified to inherit the Kramer name.
So be it.

The sun had set, and lights began to flicker through windows.

Mathias' only fear was that they might announce they were done for the evening. This didn't happen—instead, his turn came around faster than he'd anticipated.

Three soldiers sat behind the long desk. The setup allowed three volunteers to stand together before them. A bonfire crackled behind the soldiers, casting light over the volunteers' faces.

A sullen-faced soldier with striking white hair dealt with Mathias. He had to be Jörg's age, but was in far better shape. The slight redness of his nose was perhaps the result of regular drinking.

"Another refugee?"

"Yes."

As a result of conversing with the hawk-eyed youth, the man with the broad shoulders, and the plump man, Mathias had lost the nervousness he'd felt talking to people so clearly unrefined. All three had most likely had their applications accepted without a hitch. Mathias realized now that they'd been good-natured people. They'd even gone so far as to show sympathy for his plight.

"Name, age, previous employment, health issues." The white-haired soldier didn't look up from his papers.

"Kramer, Mathias. Fifteen. Previous employment…" Mathias stumbled to an unwitting halt. How to explain it? He'd never done any work per se. He accompanied his father when buying supplies…studied methods for handling negotiations…helped put documents together. What could he say to include all of that? "Um…assistant, in a merchant association. No health issues."

"Uh huh. Okay, I guess you can help with some of the logist—" For some reason the white-haired soldier broke off there and put down his pen. He peered slowly upwards. "Did you say Mathias Kramer?"

"I did."

"Hold there a moment."

The soldier got up from his seat. Keeping his eyes on Mathias, he flagged down a subordinate who was passing by and muttered something. The subordinate, also looking at Mathias now, said something in return. The white-haired soldier nodded, then came back and lowered himself into his seat. A soldier at his side with weirdly thin eyebrows peered across, looking as though he had something to add, but the white-haired soldier simply shook his head: *Leave it to me.*

Mathias balled his hands into fists. What was going on? Was there some kind of problem? Was it his age? Did he need parental consent? He'd seen other youths his age getting their applications approved without issue. Was he getting worked up over nothing?

The white-haired soldier found a document from one of the piles on the desk and, taking care to bring it up in a way that hid the contents, started to flip through the pages. Eventually his hand stopped; his eyes flicked a number of times between Mathias and the sheet. Finally, he spoke.

"I'm sorry, you'll need to go home."

Mathias' blood boiled then froze. "Huh?"

"You're not...qualified."

The soldier's tone had clearly changed. *Why?*

"That doesn't make any sense. I'm obviously in better health than the people who were just here. I saw there was a woman before me, too! You accepted her! Why won't—"

"I'm afraid I can't say. You will need to leave the line."

"The impertinence!"

Just who do you think I… Mathias had begun to say the words when it dawned on him. It wasn't that the soldier didn't know who he was. It was the other way around. It was precisely because he knew—or had been informed—who Mathias was, that he was refusing to accept the application.

"Father…"

Reading his son's thoughts was nothing for the chairman of the Kramer Merchant Association. It should have been no mystery. Hadn't Jörg's incredible talents helped him reign as one of the town's magnates?

Mathias drew a long breath, letting it slowly out.

"I understand."

"We'd welcome you, ordinarily," the white-haired soldier added, looking apologetic. "But I'm afraid the result would have been the same whoever was sitting here."

Which meant the instruction had been sent out to every section of the Garrison: *Turn down Mathias Kramer's application.* With that, Mathias knew that his plan of traveling to Quinta by joining the campaign was practically finished.

He gave the white-haired soldier a returning nod and took his leave.

The Harsh Mistress of the City

CHAPTER TWO

"Hello! Is anyone still out there?"

Rita was running between the remains of wooden structures that had burned to the ground. Fire had to be smoldering beneath the debris because it was fairly hot. The sweat was never-ending as it dripped off her. The area was filled with the tang of scorched timber and flesh.

It was nothing less than a scene from hell. Smoke billowed from charred fields in every direction. A few Titans were still there, ambling through them. The ground was peppered with holes from the bombardment. If she didn't watch out, she could stumble and fall in.

"Hello! Anybody?"

Rita squinted through piled stacks of rubble. No sign of any survivors.

She raised her head and started to run again. Her foot caught on something as she turned past one of the collapsed structures. Seeing what it was, she only just swallowed her scream.

It had once been a soldier.

The lower body, drenched with Titan saliva, had been ejected onto the ground. The upper body was nowhere to be seen. The angle thankfully hid the cross section, but Rita could glimpse where the Titan's teeth had most likely come down. The jawline was carved into the soldier's flesh, leaving the trousers soaked to the thigh in blood.

"H-Hello?! Is anyone out there?" Rita called with a trembling voice.

She had been out since morning, searching with the remaining members of the Garrison Regiment and the Training Corps for any survivors they could pull out. There had been little in the way of results. All they found were corpses spat out by the Titans or corpses that had been spat out then burned to a crisp.

"Rita, above you!"

Her eyes shot up in response to the piercing female voice. A three-meter-class was crouching in towards her, its arms wide in a trap.

"One sec…"

Instinct pushed her to reach for the mechanism to fire an anchor, but she couldn't see any solid structures nearby. She'd strayed farther from Quinta's wall than she'd thought. If she aimed at any of the charred remains, the anchor could come right off.

The Titan began a slow, lumbering fall towards her. Its abnormally hot breath blew over Rita's skin.

She rolled the moment before it had her, escaping off to one side. The giant frame crashed prone where she'd been only a moment earlier. Clouds of dust spewed into the air as the impact sent tremors through the ground and surrounding rubble.

The Titan's head jerked upwards. It planted one arm on the ground to push up its torso and reached for Rita with the other.

"Yikes. Enough!"

She readied a blade in each hand.

Just then, a shadow appeared over the Titan's frame. A female soldier landed on the Titan's sizable back and swung the two blades in her hands. Rita heard swishes of air followed by the sound of flesh being sliced open. A great curtain of steam burst from the nape of the Titan's neck. Moving quickly, the solider leapt into the air and dodged the vapor before coming to rest at Rita's side.

It was Amanda, who had graduated the same year. Rita's former classmate was tall, with straight black hair that she kept long. In terms of appearance it was fair to say she was Rita's opposite.

"Got a death wish?"

Always cool-headed, Amanda never cut anyone any slack. In this respect, too, she was more or less Rita's direct opposite. To tell the truth, Rita found her a little hard going.

"Sorry. I wasn't thinking."

"Damned inconvenient, if you went and died on us."

"Right. I'll be more careful, I swear."

"So, you noticed yet?"

Attack on Titan

Amanda's blades were locked in her hands, her eyes set on the colossal plumes of smoke funneling out from the Titan. The creatures possessed extraordinary powers of regeneration, but slice through the nape of their neck and they leaked steam from their entire body until they evaporated.

"There's no one left above us."

"Hmm?" Momentarily puzzled, Rita answered with a question. "What do you mean, no one?"

"Just that. They all got eaten, either defending the evacuees to the end or because they couldn't get back over the wall."

"Everyone?"

"Yeah. They're all dead."

"But that's…" Rita recalled the look on her commander's face as he'd given the order to shut the gate. It was true that they had yet to find any survivors outside the wall. But was it really possible that none of the officers had made it back?

"I don't believe it."

"Well, there's those who went to the other side. With the evacuees. It's what all those Military Police Brigade trash did, right?"

By "other side" she no doubt meant Fuerth. Rita turned to look down the main roadway. Scattered corpses of evacuees who hadn't been able to break free lay there too, along with their horses and the troops who had tried to protect the column. She didn't see a single living soldier. Instead she saw Titans, still wandering this way and that. What had become of Mathias? Of his father, Jörg?

"I just hope as many got away as possible," Rita said.

"If I were you, I'd put my own concerns first."

"My own concerns?" Rita cocked her head, unsure. "You mean so I don't space out, like just now? Or do you mean food?"

"Well, that too." Amanda snorted air through her nose. "But no. You're gonna be busy."

"I suppose. With fewer soldiers, we'll all have to—"

"Still not getting it. From this point on, you're in charge of the Regiment here."

"In charge? The regiment?"

Did she mean the Garrison? Rita couldn't process the information. Amanda let out an extravagant sigh.

"It's pretty obvious. When an officer dies the next in line takes over command. As things are now, there's no one above you."

"Are you sure? No one?"

"That's what I've been trying to tell you."

"But we're the same rank."

"I'm not team leader."

"True…"

It was true that, as team leader, Rita had been commanding a number of her former classmates. But that didn't mean she was any better at combat. Amanda hadn't made the position simply because her personality was seen as a problem.

"Wait. Does that mean…"

Rita made a survey of the shantytown, now just blackened fields. Young soldiers threaded paths around the trails of smoke still spiraling into the air. Granted it was only temporary, but was she really supposed to take charge of them all?

"I…can't do that! It doesn't matter what the rules say."

"It kind of does."

"You'd be much better at it than me."

"Don't be silly. Would I ever commit to something as tiresome as that?"

"But…"

"You should probably pray. That there's at least one senior officer still out there." She added, "Not that it's likely, mind."

"Oh, thanks."

In front of them the overflow of steam began to settle. The Titan was almost gone.

For there not to be a single person who ranked above her… This was only Rita's second year with the Garrison. For her to be the highest-ranking soldier!

The commanding officers must have made some kind of miscalculation. They must have believed at least one of them—someone with the proper status—had stayed behind.

"Uh, sorry, pardon me?"

Rita and Amanda swung around toward the voice. One of

the trainees had approached without their noticing—a youth with closely cropped hair. Traces of childhood innocence still played on his features. Rita seemed to remember his name was Duccio. She'd sparred with him a few times for his sake.

"We're done tending the wounded for now. Reporting in."

"Right. Thanks." Come to mention it, Rita did remember giving out the order.

"What do you want us to do now?"

"Have you checked that key personnel are safe?" Amanda said without pause.

"Don't think so."

"O-Okay, then that's next," Rita, flustered, gave the order. "Can you do that for me?"

"Would be happy to. Only, I don't know what they look like."

"Nor do I."

"Even then, that should be your job."

In response to Amanda's declaration, Rita asked, "Mine?"

"You can't have a trainee deal with the bigwigs all by himself."

"Ah… Yeah, I guess you're right." Again the thought hit Rita that Amanda was better suited for command.

Amanda only floated a sly grin, whispering as she turned away, "Don't forget your manners, madam acting commander."

"…Meanie."

Rita felt ready to cry. Instead, she ran her fingers over the

Vertical Maneuvering Equipment on her back.

Then she said to Trainee Duccio, who still looked like a kid, "Let's go. With some more people."

The district hall was completely deserted.

The stone structure, possibly the grandest in the whole of Quinta, was as silent as a graveyard. A day and a half had passed since the evacuation, or one day since they'd closed the gate. It was immediately obvious that no one had come in to work for the duration.

"It's weird though, isn't it? You'd think they'd be really busy," Duccio remarked.

A couple more trainees stood next to him. In the end Amanda had refused to join them.

"Oh?" Rita inquired.

"Absolutely. We're not going to be leaving Quinta for a while, right? There's counting how many people are still here, taking stock of how much food we've got, buying up more from people with too much. No end to what they could be doing."

"Y-Yes, of course."

Rita was still failing to appreciate the big picture. Not for the first time, she reflected on how poorly suited she was for command. Sighing, she led the three trainees up the marble staircase.

It was the first time she'd set foot in the building. There was a desk for general requests on the first floor, but Rita's mother,

Doris, had always handled tasks that involved dealing with civil servants. Everywhere above the second floor appeared to be office space for staff to complete their clerical duties. Rita doubted she would ever have come up here had circumstances been normal.

Even though the building was empty, there were no signs of it having been ransacked. Discounting the attack of the Titans, there was nothing that attested to any kind of accident or incident having taken place. Purely and simply, no one was there.

They continued down a tall-ceilinged hallway, pushed open a solid set of doors, and walked into what looked to be the district mayor's office.

It was, as expected, unmanned.

The space was fitted with a large desk and chair, along with some bookshelves, but there was no sign of the occupant. Rita recognized the faint smell of parchment.

"Think they're all at home?" Duccio wondered. "Like, maybe someone in the family got hurt."

One of the other trainees slapped the back of his head. "Yeah, right. These are the guys who gave the go-ahead for the evacuation. There's no question they were the first to hightail it out of here."

"Really?!"

"Look, we don't know that yet…" Rita tried to argue the point, but her voice tapered out. The trainee's speculation was probably accurate. It was something she hadn't even thought to consider. Noting again that she was missing the big picture, Rita felt a fresh wave of discouragement.

"But!" Duccio piped up. "If that's true, who's in charge? Of the town, and of the military? The bigwigs are all gone, right?"

"How should I know?" The other trainee folded his arms over his chest.

The third of them said, "I'm sure they're here somewhere. Just not in here."

"I hope so."

"Wait, I see," Duccio clapped his hands as though he'd just remembered something. "It'll probably be Rita, right? I mean the commander, and the person in charge of the district."

"Huh?" Rita blurted, this catching her by surprise. "D-Don't be silly. You shouldn't just say whatever comes into your head."

"But what about earlier? Ah, sorry, I kind of overheard. But that's what Amanda was saying. That Rita should be acting commander."

"For reals?"

"Ah, since all our superiors are gone…"

The trainees all looked towards Rita, their eyes full of expectation. The prospect of someone close to them becoming highly influential was, it seemed, an exciting one. All Rita wanted, meanwhile, was to be liberated from the role.

"Nothing's been decided yet. And that was just something Amanda said, with nothing to back it up."

"Maybe, but I hope it's true. You're tough as nails! I was up there, manning the cannons. I saw you out there."

"Yeah, me too."

"It was amazing. If you hadn't relayed that order, we wouldn't have gotten the gate shut in time. I bet you a few of those Titans would've gotten through."

"For sure."

The trainees nodded among themselves.

Rita felt a cold sweat creeping under her clothes. "That was just…luck. You just happened to see the best bits."

"She's modest, too!"

"Really, I can't do it. Besides, you can't decide who's acting commander based off of rank alone. There's things like experience to consider, and demeanor. It has to be someone with the right amount of gravitas."

"Come on, you've got all of that! Doesn't she, guys."

"Yup."

"We'd back you."

The three of them swapped looks, then turned to her again.

"W-We can discuss this later. First we need to check the other rooms." Thus forcing the topic to a close, Rita swiveled to face the door. She prayed to herself, *Please let there be a royal government official or a surviving Garrison officer—even just one.*

Her steps couldn't have felt heavier, but Rita started walking towards the door, somehow taking the lead. As she was about to exit into the hallway, another soldier came charging in.

"Aie, watch it!"

"Sorry!"

He was a youth, also from the Training Corps. He seemed even younger than Duccio—probably a fresh recruit, likely with next to no training. He apologized for almost crashing into her, then stood to attention, saluting with a hand over the crest adorning his chest.

"Reporting in. P-People have started looting businesses in town. H-How should we proceed?"

"Looting?!"

Incredible. It was true that the Military Police Brigade was gone, and that the Garrison had suffered devastating losses; still, could civil order break down so completely in the space of just one day?

Duccio and the others looked shaken too.

"Businesses…the ones evacuees left behind!"

"They'll have left stuff there."

"I'll come at once," Rita told the recruit. "Take me there now!"

Whatever her title, it was her duty to protect the district.

She feared for her parents.

Neither her father Henning nor her mother Doris had been part of the evacuation. They had stayed in Quinta and were keeping the apothecary open. There was no guarantee that they wouldn't be raided.

For the time being, the looting was taking place in an area that was removed from the family business. Otherwise Rita might have deployed the Vertical Maneuvering Equipment and left the trainees standing.

The disturbance had already spread over several blocks. A violent mob was sacking the many businesses lining the street. Most of the targets were, as suspected, shops whose proprietors had evacuated, but even those whose owners had stayed were being looted. On top of that, a steady influx of onlookers meant the mob was rapidly growing in size.

"That's enough! This is the Garrison Regiment. Stand back!"

Rita pushed her way past the rubberneckers. A group of men were emerging from a butchers up ahead, arms laden with rings of sausages and clumps of raw and cured meat.

"Wait!"

Rita stood blocking their way. One of the men tried to shove her aside. She tripped his leg to send him tumbling then twisted his arm in a lock. She then unsheathed one of her blades and extended it smoothly towards one of the other men.

"Put it back! Everything you've got. It's not yours to take!"

"Huh? Everyone else's doing it. It's not like they're coming back."

The man was asserting that the owners had made it past Wall

Rose and were not about to return.

"That may be the case, but it doesn't mean you—hey!" She caught another man with armfuls of meat sneaking out of the entrance. "Don't just stand there, go after him!"

"Y-Yes!"

"Sorry!"

The trainees scampered after the looter.

Rita was clenching her teeth. *There's too many…*

The looting was wholesale—at the cheese mongers next door, the greengrocers on the other side, the hardware and clothing merchants farther up. The crowd was doing nothing to stop it. If anything they looked hopeful of getting leftovers once the rough types were gone. Mixed in with the crowd, Rita caught glimpses of uniforms she recognized. Most likely they were trainees who had reached the scene before her. The looting was taking place in open view, but the recruits appeared at a loss.

"Let go of me!"

The man whose arm Rita still had in a lock began to thrash. One of the onlookers snapped up some of the meat he'd dropped. Someone else reached for him. The crowd broke into a scuffle for the meat.

"We're the Garrison Regiment! You do realize we're armed?!"

The civilians weren't listening. In fact, they seemed to have forgotten she was even there. Taking advantage of the commotion, the man broke free from under her and launched himself into the crowd. There, more fights started to get the remaining meat.

"Hey, that's enough!"

Duccio moved in to break them up but ended up getting surrounded. Elbowed in on all sides, he was about to lose his equipment.

It was hardly surprising. A recruit in his first month was little more than a novice. No one could expect him to hold his own against strong grown men.

"Don't take on more than you can handle!"

Just in the nick of time, Rita took his collar and yanked him out from the crowd.

He turned to face her, gasping for air, and asked for advice. "What now?"

"I, I think…" The odds were stacked against them. She couldn't think of a way to end the disorder without injuring any civilians.

Or maybe…that isn't true?

"Duccio, can you go and fetch guns for everyone? As many as you can carry."

"We're gonna shoot them?"

"No, we're not. The reports will do!" If they threatened the use of firepower, they might be able to disperse the mob.

"A-ha, I see!" He seemed to catch Rita's meaning. "Roger!"

"Summon everyone who's free."

"What about you?" another recruit asked Rita.

"I'll just have to do what I can here."

She was outside the butchers with a drawn blade; as could be expected, people had stopped trying to get in. She turned and took aim at a building across the street. Careful to avoid the crowd, she fired both anchors. They punctured the surface between the second and third floors. The impact vibrated down to Rita's waist.

Work with what's available. That's all I can do.

She kicked off the ground and started to reel in the wires. The belt around her body tightened and she began to rise. Her feet took to the air.

She sailed up above the crowd. They glided past the corner of her vision.

The wall was pulling closer, and fast.

She adjusted the rewinding speed. Shifting her weight, she swung her feet up towards the wall. At the moment of impact, she curved her knees and torso to absorb the tremendous force. She kicked straight back off the wall, for the moment leaving the anchors embedded in the surface. This time, she let the wires unwind slowly, thereby regulating the speed of her descent.

Below her, looters of all kinds were making their getaway, shouldering boxes and sacks filled to the brim with vegetables. Rita adjusted her posture midair and pointed her feet at the ground.

She landed right in their midst. Using both hands she held out her blades.

"This is the Garrison. Please desist from any further criminal activity."

"What?"

One of the men casually turned around.

Rita dropped into a crouch, kicking off the ground to instantly close the gap between them. Turning her wrist she drove the hilt of one of her blades into the man's solar plexus. He coughed up froth, then collapsed. His cloth sack hit the ground, scattering beans everywhere.

"Why, you little…"

One of the other men began to approach her. But he wasn't thinking straight. He was still carrying a wooden box on his shoulder.

How does he expect to fight like that?

Rita tripped his legs and he fell backwards in apparent slow motion, a bemused look on his face. His box crashed into the ground, tipping to spill potatoes.

"Holy…"

"Shit, she really is Garrison."

Some of them started to run.

Right decision.

Others had put down their loads and were making their approach.

Wrong decision.

One of them had a poker clasped in his hands. Probably something he'd used to pry open a door or a window. The bearded man brandished it upwards, then swung.

"You asked for it," Rita muttered.

She thrust her blade but pulled it back at the last moment. She wasn't out to kill anyone. The Garrison's duty was to protect *all* citizens.

She judged the trajectory of the poker and stepped to one side. She rammed the hilt of her blade into the side of the man's head as part of the same movement.

There was a sudden impact in the small of her back. She'd taken a kick from behind.

"Ow…"

She found herself stumbling forwards, but managed to keep her footing. She turned to see another man moving in, hands up before his face. He was almost in reach.

"You get special treatment!"

Without hesitation Rita fired an anchor from the mechanism around her waist. Startled, the man swayed to evade it. This much Rita had anticipated. It wasn't her intention to skewer him.

The anchor zipped through the air and stabbed into the building to his rear. Rita set the wire to rewind. A brutal force took hold of her, and she took flight at a staggering pace.

The man's eyes opened wide.

Riding the momentum of the wire Rita raised her knee, connecting it with his chin. The man flailed backwards, spurting blood from his nose as he staggered to the ground. With the attacking knee as a fulcrum, Rita executed a half front somersault to land both feet on the wall.

The rest of the men stared up at her, dumbfounded. But Rita suspected it wouldn't be long before they regained their cool. It was time to end this.

"Go home!"

She couldn't stay there on the wall forever.

As she started to fall she looked up, adjusted the angle of the firing mechanism, and fired an anchor towards another building across the street, which housed an ironmongers. She pulled the first anchor out from the wall at the same time. Yet again she sailed over the crowd below, cutting a beeline across the street.

They were becoming increasingly wary of her presence. She landed on both feet between two windows where the anchor had speared the wall. Standing perpendicular to it, she gazed down at the mob below.

"Looting is forbidden! Please desist from further criminal activity!"

She kicked off the wall again and swung into the air. She plummeted down towards a man carrying a bundle of what looked like cookery tools. Timing the blow to connect when he turned, she drove the hilt of her blade into him. He took flight, spinning multiple times before finally landing sprawled across the cobbled street.

"Sorry, but it's your own fault!"

She silently touched down.

I guess I don't need this. She re-sheathed the blade and detached the hilt, taking firm hold of the latter. Being able to fire the anchors sufficed. She didn't want to cut anyone down.

Tipping forwards, she deftly launched herself towards another group of looters. Sidestepping punches she let loose a barrage of roundhouse kicks, accelerating her heel into the sides of their heads.

"Theft is forbidden! Reinforcements are already on their way!"

She neutralized three more outside a tannery, then two outside a private home. She repeated the process outside a tavern and a tailors. From one side to the next, one building to another, Rita crisscrossed the street with lightning speed. It wasn't necessary to subdue the entire mob. Only to demonstrate military presence.

She fired an anchor into the third floor of a building markedly taller than the rest. She set the wire to reel in and pulled herself up, coming to rest on the upper ledge of a bay window. She pulled the anchor free.

Casting her eyes down to the street below, she found a man carrying a smallish leather bag. No doubt it was stolen, too. He was pushing roughly through the crowd, shoving people this way and that. Those who saw him coming were scurrying to get out of the way.

"Perfect…"

Rita reattached the hilt to her blade before pulling it from the sheath. She thrust it deep in between a couple of slats above the window. The jolt was enough to numb her arm a little. For the second time, she disconnected the hilt from the blade. Coming down into a crouch, she scanned the street and took careful aim. The man was almost directly below her now, just a little off to the right. She calibrated the angle of the mechanism and fired her anchor a meter ahead of him. He jumped and came to a full stop, almost keeling forwards. He craned his neck to see her, his face twitching in surprise.

It was the moment she'd been waiting for.

Now!

Rita fired again, this time using the anchor that had pulled her up to the building. The man's eyes opened even wider. He was frozen to the spot, his reactions lacking the necessary speed to get out of the way.

The anchor impaled his right thigh.

The man let out an ear-piercing scream. He threw the leather bag away and fell to the ground, writhing in pain.

"Sorry! But I need you…"

Rita triggered the wire to reel in, letting the compressed gas shoot out at full clip. She took the same wire and looped it over the blade she'd stuck in the wall near her feet, then jumped down on the opposite side from the man. The blade became a pivot, suspending the man to the right of the window, and Rita to the left. While she was still a little higher up, Rita depressed the trigger on the hilt of the blade to stop the wire reeling in.

She drew her second blade and pointed it towards the airborne man.

"Damn you! Argh… This bloody hurts!" Suspended with his head beneath him, red trickling down his thigh, the man thrashed around like a fish on a rod. He yelled and moaned, tears and nose running together.

Unsurprisingly, the majority of the crowd was by now looking up and watching them. Entranced by what was taking place, even the looters stood still.

"Hear me…" The words caught in Rita's throat. Hanging in midair, she sucked in a deep breath and tried again. "Hear me out. Everyone! I am…"

Right. There was no turning back now she'd come this far. She couldn't skirt around the issue any longer.

"I am Rita Iglehaut, acting commander of the Garrison. The Military Police Brigade has left to guard and escort the evacuees to safety, leaving the maintenance of law and order under the jurisdiction of the Garrison and the Training Corps!"

The reality was that the only Garrison troops left to carry out their duties were Rita herself, Amanda, and a few others from their own year and the next. The rest were all trainees with next to no experience. Rita, of course, saw no reason to volunteer that information.

"W-We! Will respond, with zero tolerance, to theft in all forms! Disband, and go home. Please go on as though everything were…"

Half of Quinta had been evacuated. The majority of its able-bodied soldiers were gone. No one could act as though nothing had happened.

Rita took a deep breath and reprised, "Inasmuch as you are able, as though everything were normal. I guarantee help *is* on its way. To enable us to make a new start in a new environment, please respect the law, and help one another!"

It struck her then that this was probably the first time she'd had to speak in front of so many people. She waited nervously for the crowd to respond.

What if they just ignore me? Dismiss me as some bubble-headed girl spouting nonsense?

There was only silence.

Then, a series of explosive bangs sounded from somewhere down the street.

Gunfire.

The people below turned in chorus. Chatter spread like a tidal wave.

Over twenty trainees were racing to the scene. They were firing repeatedly into the air to intimidate the crowd. Clouds of gunpowder smoke puffed upwards, giving the impression of greater numbers.

"Thank you…"

The looting wouldn't spread any further, at least not from here. Rita felt her tension drain away. If she weren't suspended in midair, she might have crumpled to the ground.

"You, commander? Really? I can hardly believe it." Doris made a show of rolling her eyes.

"Not commander. *Acting* commander. And you're not the only one who can't believe it."

That night, Rita sat with her parents at the dining table. Having failed to find a single surviving officer, she and her Garrison colleagues had held talks, and her capacity as acting commander had become official.

"It won't be too much of a burden?"

"It will. A heavy one… Way too heavy."

Rita was the first to agree that it felt beyond her, but without anyone to organize the soldiers, more rioting was sure to break out. That had to be avoided at any cost.

"Could you do it instead, Mom?"

"Maybe you banged your head, darling." Doris, unsurprisingly, failed to take her plea seriously.

"I give up." Rita folded her arms over the table and slumped her chin into them. "I hope the reinforcements hurry up and get here."

"I hear you."

"Still, it's hard to believe," Henning said, sipping some after-dinner tea before replacing the cup to the table. "For all the officials to just flee like that."

"Absolutely. And to think of how they always acted so important." Doris sipped her tea too and peered at Rita over the rim. "And you're doing their work, too? What does that entail?"

"I don't know yet. What do you think, Dad?" Her head was spinning from just considering it.

"Right. First, I suppose, is to make sure we know who's here. Then there's organizing a militia…as it does appear we have fewer soldiers now. Also, households with injured persons will be wanting medical attention."

"How about the stockpiles—money, supplies? Do you know how much we have left?"

Rita shook her head in response to Doris' question. "The district hall was empty. It's hard to accept, but I think—"

"The officials took them. Cretins!"

"We're lucky though, we've got the supplies the military had stored. They should be enough to last us a while."

"What about horses?" Henning asked.

"Less than twenty now."

"Could we use them to evacuate? In smaller groups?" Doris asked, clearly assuming she'd come up with a good idea.

"We thought of that but decided against it, because we'd have a hard time choosing who would go."

"Mmm, yes, I suppose."

"And…this doesn't bear thinking, but as someone pointed out, we don't really know whether the people who left actually made it through."

It wasn't impossible that they'd been wiped out. If they'd run into a group of "aberrant" Titans, some that were fast on their feet, it wasn't even all that unthinkable. Rita's mind traveled back to the innumerable dead bodies she'd had to see earlier that day, to those clumps of meat, no longer human in form, that had been chewed on and spat out by the Titans. Again, it was something that didn't bear thinking about, but no one could say Mathias and Jörg hadn't been out there among them.

"We thought it best, for now, to wait for reinforcements from Fuerth."

"Yes, you're probably right." Henning glanced at the window. The world outside was already shrouded in dark.

"I do hope the Kramers are okay," Doris muttered to herself. Her thoughts seemed to be moving in the same direction as Rita's.

"Th-They have to be. Mathias is surprisingly bullheaded, and Jörg's the shrewdest man alive!" Rita knew she wouldn't be able to stay on top of her work if she didn't keep telling herself this.

Henning floated an amused smile. "Probably best you don't say that to their faces."

"You think so?"

"I do." Henning drank up the remainder of his tea.

"Anyhow!" Doris stood and gathered their empty cups. "You need sleep if you're to have any energy for this. You *are* going to have the hardest job in the whole of Quinta."

"Don't remind me."

Even as she sat there, slumped over the table, Rita felt in her heart a powerful sense of gratitude to her parents. She could hear Doris' footsteps as she moved off to the kitchen.

"I'm sure their merchant association will commit a small fortune, buy up every last horse there is in Fuerth, and send help as soon as they can."

"Right."

Until then, she would do everything in her power to keep Quinta safe.

So that she could hold her head high when she saw Mathias again.

***

Mathias was having trouble sleeping. The rage burned deep in his chest.

He was angry with his father for making a pre-emptive move, for having seen through him—or maybe he was angry with himself for being so easy to read.

He tossed and turned. Fuerth was on higher ground than Quinta, meaning a cooler temperature. The heavy blanket felt oppressive.

His patience spent, Mathias sat up. He swung his feet to the floor and pushed his toes into icy slippers. Lighting a candle stand, he left for the kitchen to get some water.

Slivers of light trailed from the door to Jörg's chamber. Was he still working at this hour?

Mathias turned for the staircase but happened to overhear his name being spoken. His father was talking to someone about him. Like Mathias, Jörg hadn't visited the Fuerth townhouse for a long time—perhaps he'd forgotten that the walls weren't as thick as they were at the mansion in Quinta. As though compelled, Mathias began to approach his father's room.

"I understand that it's hard on the boy. I would go back too, if I could."

He had no doubt as to the identity of his father's companion. It was Suzanne, their servant and Mathias' home tutor.

Since losing his wife, Jörg often shared his bed with her. When Mathias had first discovered this—Jörg and Suzanne still didn't know he had—he'd been incensed. It had felt like a betrayal of his mother. But now he simply accepted it for what it was.

His father was human, too, and Suzanne was no doubt helping fill the void left after the passing of his wife. If they were both happy with the relationship as it was, then Mathias was fine with it.

Stilling his breath, he listened.

"But why? Is there someone you care about?"

As suspected, the voice was Suzanne's.

"Not really. Well…there are some friends, yes. And people are more important than anything else, that goes without saying—but I left certain items behind, too."

"Items?"

"I showed them to you before, remember? The artworks. I couldn't very well load them onto a wagon, not the way things were. There were so many people who couldn't evacuate. Now, that would have earned some dark looks. But even putting that aside, there was no time to haul them all out. So I left them behind."

"I'm sure you'll be able to go back."

"Not for a long time."

"Are they so valuable?"

"A significant fortune, but nothing compared to the whole. I brought everything in the way of tender. And I've always kept the majority of my assets here in the interior."

"So this is a simple question of attachment?"

"Indeed."

Mathias had, without realizing it, broken out in a sweat. He no longer felt the cold. As though he'd been sprinting at top speed, his heart was pounding hard and fast.

He's talking about…

The numerous works of art, neatly arranged in the underground room. Jörg had left them back at the Quinta mansion.

There must be some way I can use this as leverage.

Mathias' throat was drier than when he'd gotten up.

He tiptoed away from his father's chamber and slinked downstairs—the whole time fearing his thumping heart might give him away.

A bribe.

What better way was there of putting such valuable artworks to use? The question was to whom to offer them, and what to ask for in return.

Mathias tried running through it in his head.

He wanted to go back to Quinta. Once there he hoped to find Rita and, if possible, to bring her back with him to Fuerth. For that, he first needed to get past the wall. And not just get past it. He would need a horse. Without one he couldn't hope to outrun the Titans. They would devour him and he would die in vain.

He was becoming convinced that the only way to get past the wall with a steed was to join the campaign to retake Shiganshina.

Yet the sections responsible for drafting volunteers had been issued orders not to accept him. In the end, it seemed to him that his only course of action was to bribe one of the soldiers signing people up.

Clearly, he couldn't just approach the desk and say, "Sign me up and I'll tell you where to find some treasure." For one thing, there was no guarantee that the soldier in question would be the kind that was receptive to bribery. All of which meant that he had to find…

"A place where corrupt soldiers hang out, huh."

The day after he'd listened in on his father's conversation, Mathias spent the afternoon quietly at home in the townhouse. Come evening, he changed into the plainest clothes he could find. He told Suzanne he wouldn't need dinner, then hurried out before anyone asked any questions.

He headed first in the direction of the Garrison barracks. From there he visited every store and food hall in the vicinity, plying the same made-up story to gather information on all the cheap taverns in the neighborhood: *You don't know any of the soldiers' taverns, do you? Since my brother joined the Garrison he's been out drinking every night. Mom's beside herself…*

He was fortunate in that everyone he spoke to was sympathetic. Some of the women even went as far as to show concern: *Of course…but promise me you'll be careful. It's an unsavory crowd there.*

Attack on Titan

For Mathias' purposes, the more unsavory the places were, the better. That only increased his chances of finding soldiers of dubious moral character. He finally decided on one hidden deep in a complex web of back alleys, relatively far away from the barracks. By then the sky had turned completely dark.

He did hesitate outside the entrance, but this lasted only seconds. Whatever the nature of the clientele, they would be nothing compared to a gaggle of Titans. He wouldn't be devoured head first.

The din and heat seared out the moment he opened the door. It was abnormally hot inside, with enough vapor and smoke to obscure the recesses from sight. The tavern was larger than he'd expected; the seating seemed to continue beyond the wall visible up ahead. Shabby male servers were busy pushing through the crowd. Mathias couldn't see any waitresses. Perhaps you had to be a man to handle a crowd this rough.

From what he could see, most of the seats were taken up by uniformed men. It did appear to be a hangout for soldiers. It also seemed the kind of place where barely educated characters came to blow off steam. Somewhere where the main purpose was to get drunk and make noise, not to enjoy quick-witted conversation or debate.

A lesson of sorts.

The experience might prove useful one day. Still, it wasn't really the kind of place he'd want to visit often. He already didn't care to breathe too much.

"Hm…" He wasn't sure where to sit, even whether he was supposed to choose a seat. Either way, none of the servers had spared him a glance.

Mathias decided to try moving farther in. He had feared that he'd stick out, that he'd be too conspicuous, but it looked as if he needn't have worried. No one was paying any attention to anyone else. The soldiers guzzled booze. Gnawed at cooked meat. Howled with laughter at vulgar jokes. Some of the tables were sprawled with cards, with copper and silver coins piled in front of the occupants. They seemed to be involved in some kind of gambling.

To order…it apparently sufficed to flag down a server at random and to shout out the menu item.

Mathias tried waving his hand at one of them. The server's only response was to nod. Apparently this meant: *Hold on, I'll be right back*.

That would do. He approached one of the tables where people were gambling. Four men sat glaring at the cards in their hands.

Here too, Mathias aimed for an attitude that would be firm but not antagonistic.

"Pardon me. May I?"

"Huh?"

One of the men looked up. The stink of booze wafted over

Mathias' face.

"Are you free to talk?"

The man frowned and clucked his tongue, then turned back to his cards as if Mathias didn't even exist.

Maybe that wasn't the smartest thing to do, Mathias admitted. He doubted anyone interrupted in the middle of a game with stakes would react well. *I'll watch for now.* He took a step backwards. He took care not to bump into any of the passing servers.

Standing in their way was dangerous.

Moving to a corner of the room, he pressed his back to the wall. He heard a whistle. Looking up, he saw the server from earlier sending him an expectant look from behind one of the tables. He wanted to know Mathias' order.

"Ale!" It wasn't like he'd never tried the stuff before.

He thought he'd shouted, but the surrounding racket drowned him out. The skin-headed server raised a hand to his ear. Mathias assumed this meant that the man couldn't hear him.

Friendlier than expected, Mathias happily noted.

He pointed at a nearby table then at himself, motioning that he wanted what they were having. The server returned a diligent nod then moved away, the message apparently having got across. Mathias surveyed the tavern again.

He'd been far too careless earlier. He couldn't proposition just any soldier. It had to be someone of dubious moral character who also wielded enough clout to sneak Mathias in as a volunteer.

He looked around for soldiers who seemed high in rank. Were there any who were impressively decorated or acting self-important and bossing others around?

His eyes came to rest on one face in particular.

Someone from the volunteer desk the previous day. Not the soldier who had dealt with Mathias, but the one who had attended to the right-hand queue. The stocky one with the thin eyebrows. Mathias was sure of it.

He walked cautiously over.

The man was playing a game of dice. Apparently down on his luck, he had been banging copper and silver coins down on the table for some time. These were, without fail, scooped up by the rest of the soldiers. The man continued to guzzle one drink after another, firing curses at the servers and the others at the table. No one seemed to take offense. Far from it, they all gave the impression of being in high spirits. Mathias guessed the soldier with the thin eyebrows had already parted with a considerable sum of money.

Eventually, the soldier got up from his seat. Maybe to use the toilet.

Perfect. Mathias pushed forwards, weaving his way past tables. Trailing after the man, he crossed a doorless threshold into a narrow, dingy-looking corridor. "Excuse me!" he called.

"Huh?" The soldier turned around and scowled, but continued, "Hey…wait a minute. Don't I know you?"

"Do you have a moment to talk?"

"Ah, I remember. The spoiled brat."

Blood surged to Mathias' head.

Let it go. He couldn't let himself get worked up each time someone from the laboring classes muttered something he found offensive. He took a lungful of the dingy air.

Tobacco, drink, paraffin, the stink of unbrushed teeth.

"That's right," Mathias said. "And the spoiled little brat has a favor he wants to ask."

"Forget it." The soldier with the thin eyebrows propped himself against the wall and scratched his head. The sense was returning to his eyes. He was, it seemed, already beginning to sober a little. "Get yourself home, go back to your lessons."

"You need to hear me out."

"Yeah? And why's that? It's obvious what you're gonna ask."

It was that damn notice.

Still—the fact that the soldier was so quick to pick up on this meant he might be of the necessary rank to grant Mathias' request. At the very least, the odds were high that he could. Mathias drew in another lungful of the filthy air.

"I can make it worth your while."

Go on, it's the next step that counts. You don't need to feel intimidated by one paltry soldier...

"I have information. I assume you know who my father is? If you agree to help, I will tell you the location of a fortune he has hidden away. And how to steal it."

"A-ha!" The soldier's eyes lit up. "Come on then, let's hear it."

"First you give me your word. That you'll enroll me as a volunteer. That you'll forge whatever documents are necessary and—"

The soldier moved before Mathias could even finish. One of his beefy arms came lunging out. His hand locked around Mathias' neck, pushed him against the wall, then lifted him bodily off the ground.

Mathias was choking from the pressure. His vision started to fade. He barely had any idea what had happened.

"W…ait…" He tried swinging an arm, but the soldier's face and body were out of reach. Mathias writhed and kicked at the man's knees, but he was like a stone column. "What…"

"How about you tell me where it is? That hidden fortune. Seems a pretty sweet deal," the soldier with the thin eyebrows rasped.

"Only…in…exchange…"

"Don't be a dolt. This is life or death. The only sensible choice is to spit it out, and fast."

"If you…kill…"

"Hmm?" The soldier flashed a false smile, cocking his head to one side. "There'd be one less idiotic kid, that's all. It's common knowledge you were trying to get past the wall. Who knows why? Not that it matters. Anyway, wouldn't be no surprise if you got

109

washed up in the river."

Of course.

Mathias hadn't thought about the river. It ran the length of Fuerth before passing under the wall, through to the outside. And Quinta was downstream. Forgetting a steed, assuming he could hold his breath long enough, it wouldn't be inconceivable to dive in and leave that way.

"You understanding yet? I strangle you here, and splash! Everyone'll assume you drowned. No skin off my nose."

The man's grip tightened around Mathias' neck. No doubt the soldier meant it. The drink, combined with all the money he'd lost, had pushed him out of control. Mathias could tell the soldier wouldn't hesitate to kill him.

"Spit it out. The hidden fortune. Look, I'll even consider splitting the proceeds."

"Well, that does sound interesting. Perhaps you'd consider enlightening me," came another male voice, this one with an odd affectation. The pitch was almost musical. "Only me, of course."

The very next moment, the soldier with the thin eyebrows rolled his eyes backwards and collapsed to the floor, and the pressure around Mathias' throat was abruptly gone.

Mathias followed the man to the ground and landed on all fours, retching. It wasn't until a dozen shallow breaths later that he finally realized what had happened. Through teary eyes he peered up to see a tall soldier sporting a mustache. At least, the man was dressed like a soldier, and he had to be the source of the last utterance.

He looked around thirty. Yet Mathias would have believed he was fifty, if someone had told him so. The mustache made it hard to tell the man's true age.

"A good evening to you. Mathias Kramer, I presume?"

Mathias had been right, the man's speech was oddly affected. The man proffered a hand. He seemed to want to help up the junior Kramer.

For a moment, Mathias wasn't sure if he should take it.

What if this man turned out to be like the soldier with the thin eyebrows? More to the point, how did he know who Mathias was?

"Nice work, boss. Nice and clean."

Another soldier approached from behind. This one was old, but he was big and covered in burly muscle.

Mathias wondered for a moment if he might be hallucinating, but the more he looked at the soldier's face, the more elderly he seemed. His cropped hair was silver and streaked with white. Mathias had never seen an old man so powerfully built.

Two more soldiers filed in behind him. They wore brand-new uniforms. One was a boy who looked no older than Mathias. The other was an even younger—no, a young woman.

Mathias was beginning to feel confused.

None of them indicated surprise at the scene before them, at finding the soldier with the thin eyebrows sprawled unconscious over the floor of the corridor. Were they all aware that he had attacked Mathias?

"That should go without saying. I am quite proficient," the mustached soldier said in a singsong tone. "Come, to your feet!" He extended his hand even farther.

With nothing else to do, Mathias clasped hold of it and let himself be pulled up. He was still a little dizzy. He put his hand on the wall to steady himself.

"How do you know who I am?"

"How do I know you? My friends, did you hear that?"

He glanced back at the soldiers behind him. The gigantic old man wore a big grin; Mathias got the impression that the man was always smiling. The boy was looking coldly away. The woman upturned a tankard of what was probably ale and narrowed her eyes in apparent bliss. The mustached soldier turned back towards Mathias.

"How would I not know the scion of the renowned Kramer Merchant Association?"

Perhaps they had also seen Jörg's notice, the one containing the message to turn down Mathias' application. Perhaps they'd been there watching when he was rejected. Still, the soldier's phrasing suggested he'd known Mathias from before the notice had gone out.

"It was clear the moment you came in. The abundant

intellect! The oozing refinement! How out of place you were in a cesspool like this. An ill-match indeed!"

The gigantic old man was still grinning. The boy tutted, and the woman stifled a yawn.

The others addressed the mustached soldier as "boss" but didn't seem to be treating him in accordance with the title.

"You were watching me? The whole time?" Mathias inquired of the mustached soldier.

"Naturally."

"Then you also overheard our exchange?" Mathias glanced at the soldier with the thin eyebrows still recumbent on the floor.

"Assuredly. Hence our decision to intervene," the mustached soldier said. He suddenly swung his head in closer. "Which brings me to my next question. It appears you are in possession of some rather special information?"

"Ah, um…" Mathias inevitably felt cautious. He couldn't afford to make the same mistake twice.

"I ask that you give us a chance. You wish to volunteer for the campaign to take back Shiganshina?"

"Yes. But who are you all?"

They seemed awfully familiar with the way of the world.

Despite their air of having seen many battles, all four had only simple marks on their collars. It was hard to believe they exercised any influence over personnel decisions.

"Oh, we're just a group of humble volunteers. Who have

only just obtained their uniforms. Still, I can't help but think we might be the most appropriate people to help you with your arrangements. I can assure you we're a fair amount more pliable than regular soldiers." He cast a look over his shoulder and exchanged a knowing smile with the gigantic old man. "And perhaps we should change venue. To some place more suitable for private discourse."

The mustached soldier proffered his hand for a second time, forcing it into Mathias' own. "Call me Bernhardt. It's a good name, no? Nothing like yours, but it does have a certain dignified ring to it."

Not in my book, Mathias felt an urge to argue, but decided to keep his mouth shut.

Who were these people? These terribly shady people?

Mathias followed the group, having resigned himself to whatever might happen. The mustached soldier—Bernhardt—flagged down a server, thrust a number of silver coins into his palm, and requested a private room.

The room was cramped, with a round table in the center and six chairs around it. Although it was only separated from the nearby hall by a flimsy wall, the outside clamor dropped away the instant the door was closed.

Mathias had finally claimed his drink from the server. Bernhardt and the others also had drinks before them.

Bernhardt raised his aloft. "To our meeting!"

Nobody followed his cue. As for the woman, she had already started imbibing a new one. Bernhardt shrugged, finished the gesture alone, then took a deep gulp of the ale.

"We should continue our introductions. The large one over there is Jarratt."

"Good to meet you, kid." A giant arm stretched out.

Not knowing what else to do, Mathias took the man's hand and shook it. "You too," he said.

The gigantic old man, Jarratt, flashed a toothy smile. A great many creases formed next to his eyes. He seemed good-natured—rather relentlessly so.

"The sulky one is Klaus. The rose among us weeds, Nikki."

Klaus gave Mathias a brief, moody glance, but looked away almost immediately. Mathias didn't remember having done anything to offend him. Klaus most likely bore him a natural aversion. Maybe he was the type who considered everyone in the privileged classes his enemy.

Meanwhile, Nikki seemed utterly disinterested in him. She gazed fondly at her tankard, pouring and gulping down drink after drink.

"I..."

"We're a charming bunch, wouldn't you agree?"

"I'll need to know more than just your names."

"Mmm. As in, what we can do. Whether we can help grant

you your wish. This is what you want to know?"

"And what you do, or what you used to do, that sort of thing…"

"Let's just say we are engaged in a rather special line of work."

"You're not soldiers?"

"This is but a temporary guise. The truth is—we are artists."

"Except, we're actually just thieves," corrected Nikki.

Jarratt's huge frame rocked with laughter. Bernhardt leveled the young woman with a reproachful look.

"'Thieves'—how atrocious. Am I not always telling you to at the very least refer to ourselves as being 'outlaws'? Add 'glorious' before it and all the better. *Glorious outlaws.*"

"Sorry, hold on. You're thieves?"

"Yeah. Glorious thieves," replied Nikki.

"Not thieves, *outlaws*. Glorious outlaws!"

"Except in your case, boss, maybe 'small-time crook' is more like it."

Jarratt cackled with laughter, and Klaus muttered after him, "Or 'dingy ex-soldier.'"

"Soldier? You said those are temporary guises, but you used to be in the military?"

"A lifetime ago, yes." Bernhardt shrugged. "I used to be in the Military Police Brigade."

"Military Police Brigade? *The* Military Police Brigade?"

Only the highest achievers from the Training Corps were able to join them. What was a member of that elite group doing as a thief?

"Got caught, didn't he," Nikki divulged with a mischievous grin. "Rerouting supplies to the black market, turning a blind eye to smuggling."

Bernhardt snorted. "It's my policy not to dwell on the past."

"Right… I suppose there are all those stories of corruption in the Brigade." Mathias examined the mustached soldier, Bernhardt, with renewed appreciation. It was the first time he'd met a true-to-life corrupt soldier.

"I do find 'corruption' such a distasteful word. I was a little more pliable than most, that is all."

"So the rest of you are all people he got to know during his…"

"Yup," Nikki spoke up. "In exchange for the odd gift here and there, Bernhardt kindly turned a blind eye to our activities."

"Or gave us the times and locations of new shipments," contributed Jarratt.

They really were outlaws. The kind of people who saw fit to steal other people's possessions and to sell on the goods for profit. It was obvious they couldn't be trusted. They absolutely couldn't be trusted… But Mathias was looking for troops of dubious moral character who would be open to bribery. If anyone was suitable for the task at hand, it was them.

"Is it okay for you to just…come out and tell me you're

outlaws?"

"We would have told you eventually. Let's just say we've saved ourselves a little bother, shall we?" Bernhardt spread his arms wide. "At least now you'll understand. We are experts when it comes to tiptoeing under the nose of the royal government. At the moment, we also happen to be soldiers. Can you think of anyone better qualified to serve your needs?"

"No, I suppose not. But why did people like you think to volunteer?"

"For the good of humanity, of course."

Nikki creased up at her own words, but Bernhardt gainsaid her. "Many people had to leave their fortunes behind during the evacuation. To this side of Wall Rose. Meaning there are hordes of abandoned treasure lying unattended in towns and villages between Wall Rose and Wall Maria."

"So we go in and reap the harvest." Jarratt winked at Mathias. The little touch hardly suited the gigantic old man.

"I see..." This was looking better and better for Mathias. "Then I think we should be able to work together. That sounds perfect."

"How so?" Nikki leaned in, suddenly beaming. Her behavior seemed to change profoundly depending on whether she was interested or not.

"Part of my father's fortune, a collection of valuable artworks, is still back in Quinta."

"Bingo!" Bernhardt slapped a hand on his thigh. "I had wondered if it was. I've known for quite some time that your miser of an old man... Pardon me, that he has been a collector of such things."

"How?"

"The military police are very close with merchant associations. You don't appear to remember, but you and I actually met some years ago."

"We did?"

"Only in passing, of course."

In recent years, Mathias had often accompanied Jörg on his trips away for business. If Bernhardt really had been with the military police, then there was nothing particularly surprising about them having crossed paths.

"That's how you knew it was me the moment I came in here."

"To new friends and continued relationships!" Bernhardt raised his tankard dramatically into the air once again.

Mathias paid this no attention. "Okay, you've convinced me. Going back to what I said earlier, will you be able to get me there? To Quinta."

"Ah, you want to reach Quinta, not simply get outside of the wall."

"Yes."

"May I enquire as to why?"

"We've told you about us. Your turn," Jarratt said, with foam from the ale stuck to his mouth.

"Well…" If he told them his real reason, would they believe him? Even if they did, they would surely just make fun of him.

"A lady, perhaps?" Bernhardt said without any warning.

Mathias' face flushed red. He found himself swallowing hard.

"Of course, I see." Bernhardt emptied his tankard and slammed it back onto the table. "Wonderful! It seems that our new friend here is in love!"

"No, that's not it. Please."

"Oh, you've no reason to be ashamed. No need to be shy, either. There truly is nothing as wonderful as being in love!"

"This treasure. Where in Quinta is it?" Klaus asked.

"I can't tell you yet." They might dispose of him if he told them now. Or at least, they would have no reason to lead him outside of the wall. "I'll tell you once we're there," Mathias promised.

"You'll slow us down."

"That might be true, but…"

"Maybe the treasure doesn't even exist. Maybe it's all one big lie."

"I'm not making this up!" Mathias was on his feet before he even realized it himself. His chair capsized noisily backwards.

"That will do, you two," Bernhardt intervened, and Nikki frowned next to him as though offended by all the commotion.

"Isn't it worth taking a look, though?" Jarratt smiled in Klaus' direction. "We'll be heading out either way. And we'll need to get supplies at some point. It shouldn't be any great hassle to make a little diversion down to Quinta."

"If you're lying, you're dead," Klaus threatened, his voice low.

Coming out in a cold sweat, Mathias repeated, "I'm not making this up. And I won't slow you down."

And don't let your guard down for an instant. Always remain suspicious, he warned himself.

***

Rita was dreaming. It was a dream she used to have regularly, but this was the first time in a while.

In it, she was standing motionless in the doorway to a room she didn't recognize. Sunlight streamed through the windows, but the room was shockingly dark.

There was a table inside. Some chairs.

Against the wall was a shadow of a person. A grown man. He was crouched down, huddled into a ball.

Rita began to approach. Her vantage point was low. She was still a kid, younger yet than when she and Mathias had first met.

Gently, she placed a hand on the man's back. It felt terribly insubstantial. For some reason, it lacked any warmth.

The man must surely have noticed her. But he wouldn't turn around.

She caught sight of his profile. It was a face she'd seen somewhere before. One she thought she knew well… Yet she couldn't bring to mind the person it belonged to. It felt like the memory had simply chosen to abandon her.

Was it Henning as a younger man?

Or Mathias as an older one?

—*Neither.*

The man cradled a wooden box in his arms. More precisely, he was leaning on it. The man's body was limp. Perhaps he was asleep.

Rita noticed something.

On the wooden floor next to the man's feet was a small vial about the size of a thumb. A few drops remained inside. A transparent liquid.

Rita picked it up. She began to scrutinize it. Then she shifted her attention back to the man and tried shaking him by the shoulder.

He didn't wake.

Deep was his love for the wooden box—deep.

Rita caught a faint smell of decay.

The Harsh Mistress of the City

CHAPTER THREE

Unexpectedly, their departure came in the morning.

"Our goal is to help people nearby. We wouldn't be able to find anyone at night, even if there were people out there. Isn't that so," Bernhardt, who stood next to Mathias, observed in his usual singsong manner.

"I suppose…"

A few hundred soldiers were already gathered before the gate. Around a tenth were regulars, and the rest were volunteers. The former were on horseback, while the latter were grouped in so many wagons.

Mathias and the others were in the wagons. Mathias shared one with Bernhardt and Nikki, while Klaus and Jarratt rode in another.

In charge of Mathias' vehicle was a sloppily dressed middle-aged soldier whose skin had somehow remained supple. He'd been yawning for a while and looked half-asleep. Despite this, the fellow was kitted out with a set of the Vertical Maneuvering Equipment, with launchers and sheaths for his blades slung over either side of his waist. Mathias couldn't help wondering if the man really was proficient in its use.

"You were lucky. For that man to let you take his place so quickly."

"Hm. Yes."

Mathias' response to Nikki, who sat facing him, ended up sounding half-hearted because in the end, they hadn't needed to bribe any of the soldiers in charge of signing up volunteers.

They'd gotten Mathias in as follows: First, they'd spoken to a random volunteer, paying him an upfront fee. Next, before they were due to leave, they'd paid him the remaining sum in exchange for his equipment and badge. Finally, they'd watched him disappear into a back street.

There had been little risk of being turned down since the volunteers were mostly in it for the money. During the evacuation from Quinta, many of them had seen the Titans. A number had developed second thoughts and dropped out of the campaign even before passing through the gates.

"If I'd known it would be this easy, I'd have managed it by myself," Mathias blurted out his complaint.

Overhearing, Bernhardt gave a despairing shake of his head. "Such folly…" He brought his head in uncomfortably close and continued in a whisper, "How would you have reached Quinta, if you'd been on your own? You have no horse, and you lack the guile to rob one from the soldiers. Even supposing you did break away, you would be nothing more than a meal."

"Yes, maybe," Mathias conceded the point. "Plus, I can't ride."

"You *can* use a gun, right?" Nikki asked.

"A bit. My father showed me how."

"A very good decision." Bernhardt sat back, his voice no longer hushed. "The rich often find themselves gaining the antipathy of the poor. And you have a good chance of being robbed. A gun is necessary for your own protection."

"But surely these aren't any good against the Titans." Mathias glanced at his allocated weapon. The gun had two side-by-side barrels. The design meant it could fire a couple of shots in quick succession.

"Your folly knows no bounds," Bernhardt lamented with another extravagant shake of his head. "Your gun fires buckshot. True, this doesn't help against a ten-meter-class, but it's perfectly serviceable for blinding a five-meter-class. Guns are for more than simply killing the enemy."

"Oh, really?"

Mathias hadn't seen any Titans during his evacuation from Quinta. His party had left long before their arrival.

He'd only ever seen a Titan in person once.

A few years ago, a connection of his father's had enabled him to visit the top of Wall Maria. From there, he had gazed down at the world beyond. He'd espied a lone seven-meter-class, only barely visible in the distance, but even then it had been a substantial shock. For a while afterwards, recalling the image at night, he'd been unable to sleep.

"Use your imagination!"

Bernhardt was in high spirits. The thought of venturing beyond the wall didn't appear to worry him in the slightest. The same seemed to be true for Nikki, as well as Jarratt and Klaus. Their nonchalant attitude stood out among the volunteers, all of whom wore tense expressions. It was no great surprise that many were withdrawing from the campaign.

"We're not going today, then. To Quinta."

"The district has the wall," Bernhardt said. "They've judged that Quinta can fend for itself for a while. Our first duty is to reconnoiter the land between Wall Rose and Wall Maria and to save anyone still living there. The judgment itself is sound."

"I guess it does make sense."

It was as Mathias had heard the day before. The royal government betrayed no concern for the people stuck in Quinta. Their main priority was to reclaim Shiganshina.

"And yet you are impatient to be reacquainted with your lady friend. That is where we enter the equation."

"Hey, it's opening," Nikki indicated, a bounce in her voice.

All eyes turned to the gate. The great chains began to roll, hauling the iron-reinforced portals open. Light began to filter through the inside portion of the cave-like passageway. A commotion stirred among the ranks of volunteers, and many were holding their hand over their mouths, as though to stifle an urge to throw up. Some were pale-faced and shaking, while others were pleading with the regular troops to close the gate again. No doubt memories of being attacked by the Titans were beginning to resurface.

At the front of the crowd, the commanding officer of the rescue operation seemed to be making a speech. A short while later, an authoritative rallying cry rang into the air.

Bernhardt happily announced, "We're off!"

The wagon lurched forwards with a start. Mathias came dangerously close to toppling off it. He gritted his teeth and hung on desperately to the lip of the vehicle. The up-down motion was worse than he'd expected. He had to be careful not to bite off his tongue.

"Here's to getting rich," Nikki said, sounding blasé as she sat opposite fiddling with her rifle.

The first village rolled into view after a couple of hours on the road.

It was built around a bridge crossing the river. Relatively large, it had acted as a transport hub due to its position intersecting two main routes. Wooden houses lined the main street, while the thatched roofs of various one-story structures dotted the grasslands and hills nearby.

No Titans appeared to be in the area. Mathias had to wonder

whether less had made it through Shiganshina than they'd initially feared.

His optimism was painfully short-lived.

"What the…"

The closer they got, the more the air began to reek—with the smell of decomposition, mixed with that of excrement and an acrid accent reminiscent of vinegar.

Soon enough, the origin became apparent.

The villagers' corpses lay strewn over the main road and the fields nearby. None retained their original shapes. Each had had their limbs severed. Their bones and viscera, exposed. Every last one was slathered with translucent mucus.

"Titan spit," was all Bernhardt said.

The Titans gorged themselves on people. Yet this action had no relation to sustenance. They chewed flesh and bone then casually spat them out. Even now, it was not known how they sustained their enormous frames.

The march of the rescue force came to a halt before the village threshold. Progressing any farther would mean crushing the bodies under horse and wagon. The commanding officer seemed to have qualms about doing so.

"Just get on with it," Klaus muttered. His and Jarratt's wagon had stopped directly in front of the one containing Mathias and the others.

"Makes you wanna gag," Nikki said, using a cloth to cover

her nose and mouth.

His resolve apparently set, the commanding officer issued his orders. "C-Continue forwards! All units, I want thorough searches of each building. Look for survivors!"

The wagons began to shunt forwards. Wheels climbed onto corpses, the weight crushing them with loud cracks. The sensation rode up through the floor to where Mathias sat. As Nikki had said, it was enough to make him gag.

Bernhardt slapped him on the back. "A little fortitude, son."

The impact made Mathias want to throw up his guts.

Here and there, soldiers were pulling their horses to a stop. Volunteers were jumping down from the wagons to search the buildings. Someone shrieked after misstepping to land on one of the corpses.

The majority of the regulars remained on their horses. No doubt it was so they could stay alert, and to set the wagons running should something go wrong. And yet the wagons were too closely packed for that. If they did try to flee, they would just crash into one another.

"Should we try searching somewhere else?" Bernhardt, perhaps worried about this, called out to the soldier in charge of their wagon.

The middle-aged soldier with supple skin shot him a suspicious look. "Hunh?"

"The buildings are crowded together here. The Titans would

Attack on Titan

have targeted this area first." Bernhardt motioned his chin down one of the side roads. "We're here to find survivors. I think we might do better over there. The house on top of that hill. It looks like there could be people inside that one."

The soldier gazed at the structure. Whether or not there were survivors, there were far fewer bodies on the ground. The smell would be better too.

He nodded, pulling his eyebrows into a scowl. "Yes, agreed. We can go there."

"Not alone, though?" Bernhardt said, glancing at the wagon ahead.

Jarratt seemed to be making a point to his own wagon's trooper. It seemed the old man had understood Bernhardt's intention and was suggesting the same.

The two soldiers exchanged glances then nodded in unison.

"We can both go," the soldier with the supple skin said. He pulled on the reins and turned the horse around.

Trampling and riding over bodies as they went, the two wagons proceeded past the rows of buildings and up the hill. They finally came to a stop at the house, which consisted of a main building, a barn-like structure, and an outhouse. As expected there were no corpses in the area. The horrific stench was also mostly gone.

"Go take a look around."

Urged by the soldier, Mathias and company stepped down

132

from their wagons. It was humiliating to be bossed around by a low-ranking grunt, but Mathias supposed that this, if any, was the time for "a little fortitude."

Underfoot he felt the earth and the grass.

"Ah—how we underlings must suffer!" Bernhardt said, cheerful and not looking the slightest bit put out.

Together, the five of them headed towards the house.

"We should split up for the search."

In line with Bernhardt's instructions, Mathias and Nikki stepped into what seemed to be the main building. The air carried the smell of dust.

"Hello? We're here to help. Are there any survivors?" ventured Mathias, but there was no response. There was nothing to suggest that the place was inhabited. He stayed alert as he explored, but the bare-floored room and kitchen were both empty. The owners had either fled or been snapped up by the Titans.

"When are we going to break away?" Mathias addressed Nikki's back.

They didn't have time to be making a serious search for survivors. They needed to get clear of the rescue force as soon as possible, to make haste for Quinta.

Nikki answered over her shoulder, "No good comes from being impatient."

"But I *am* impatient!"

"Bernhardt will make good on his word. First, we've got work to do."

She was examining shelves, the insides of pots.

"Ah, I see…"

They had never intended to look for survivors, but only to take for themselves any supplies the residents had left behind. A place like this was sure to have all kinds of cured meats, cheeses, oils, and booze for the finding. Mathias felt a sudden rush of anxiety—could he really place his trust in this bunch?

"Everyone, over here!" a shout came from outside. It was Jarratt.

Nikki pulled her head out of a storage bin and peered out of the window. "Was that someone calling?"

"I think so. Although it didn't sound particularly urgent."

"Righty-ho. Let's go see."

They walked out from the main building. The voice had seemed to come from somewhere inside the barn-like structure. The supple-skinned soldier had dismounted and was also moving in to investigate. Mathias and Nikki joined him, circling around, and entered.

"Wow…"

They could see it immediately. The place was a stable. Tied up within an enclosed space were two cows, imposingly big. The feed and water troughs were both empty, suggesting they hadn't been fed in a while. The air was putrid. A mountain of excrement had piled up beneath the two animals.

Mathias had to face away.

Jarratt and Bernhardt were standing next to each other, right up against the enclosure. They seemed bewitched by the animals, apparently unaware of the offensive smell.

"This…is an amazing find," the soldier with the supple skin breathed, staring wide-eyed.

Nikki swallowed audibly. "Enough for…how many meals?"

It was only then that Mathias understood. The cows were indeed a tiny fortune. They could be eaten, or maybe even milked.

"Think we could transport them?" the soldier asked no one in particular.

"Think about it," Bernhardt calmly pointed out. "They're too big. The wagons wouldn't hold them, and even if they could, we'd be too slow to outrun any Titans that might appear."

"We could let them go, if that happened."

"And how many seconds would you waste doing that? How many tens of seconds? If a seven-meter-class takes one step for every second, how much would it gain on us in, say, five seconds?"

"Damn it," the soldier cursed, irritated. His hand tightened over the hilt of one of the blades around his waist.

"Be lighter if we butchered them," Jarratt said, extending a hand through the enclosure to stroke one of the cows on the head.

"Butcher them?" Mathias echoed.

Everyone was staring at Jarratt. The gigantic old man simply shrugged. "Used to be in the business. 'Course, if we do that we wouldn't be able to milk them and all. But if we take the meat and the skin, get rid of everything else…"

"That would make it somewhat lighter." Bernhardt considered the matter, brushing his hand over his chin.

Nikki cut in. "Wouldn't that take ages?"

"Two hours would be enough."

Bernhardt raised an eyebrow. "Two hours per cow, you mean."

"I could show you how to do it, boss," Jarratt said matter-of-factly. "Wouldn't be a problem if you stood next me, followed what I did. There's a bit of a knack, sure, but you'd be fine. You are after all a master when it comes to flaying flesh," the old man reminded with a chuckle.

Mathias recalled that Bernhardt had been in the Military Police Brigade. The man was accustomed to special blades and knew all there was to know about wielding them to fight the Titans. Apparently, the only way to slay one was to slice a vertical chunk of flesh from the nape of its neck. If Bernhardt boasted such know-how, then perhaps, at least compared to an amateur like Mathias, butchering a cow was an easy task for him.

"I see—good thinking. Would you be happy for us to do that?" Bernhardt checked with the soldier.

"Butchering the cattle, huh…"

"First we'll need to get them outside. It's difficult to move in here, and the stink won't have anywhere to go," Jarratt said.

"Get them outside?" Mathias found himself asking.

"Of course." Jarratt was already opening the gate to the enclosed space. "See that rope? Fetch it this way. Never know when they might start to struggle. Loop it around the neck, like so…"

Everyone followed the former butcher's instructions and led the first cow out of the stable. Klaus, who had been away investigating the outhouse, rejoined them partway through. Even he stared in amazement when he heard their plan.

The cow just ambled forward, shaking its head like it was being tickled by the sunlight. It blew air through its nose.

To think of me helping transport beef… Until the previous day Mathias had spent his time in the Kramer townhouse, and now, in a corner of a village cluttered with corpses, he was shooing an excrement-covered cow with a band of former outlaws. Even a week ago, he would never have imagined doing anything like this.

A little fortitude, he repeated to himself.

They encircled the cow outside the stable. Only the second serviceman remained away from the group. He was apparently keeping watch over the wagons.

"Good. Now hold it steady, both sides. Not so tight. Good… Would someone pass me a gun?" His eyes fixed on the cow's, Jarratt turned his right hand so its palm faced upwards.

"Is this okay?" Mathias hurried to hold out his weapon.

Jarratt gave it a quick look, then shook his head. "Best we don't use buckshot."

"Take this." Nikki took her rifle from the leather belt slung over her back and held it out towards the gigantic old man.

"Perfect." Jarratt took the weapon and held it ready, positioning the muzzle over the middle of the animal's forehead.

"How wonderful. To be blessed with such talented friends!" Bernhardt gestured towards Jarratt as though introducing him to some unseen audience.

The others were watching with bated breath. The cow slathered its long tongue around its mouth, showing no awareness of its impending doom. All eyes were focused on it.

So many eyes…

Abruptly, Mathias was seized by a feeling that something was wrong. He looked up.

His heart almost stopped.

They had all been in danger of losing their lives before the cow. An enormous human face larger than the animal peeked over the roof of the main building.

A Titan.

The baby-faced creature had both hands clamped on the roof. Showing itself only from the nose upwards, it was watching Mathias and the others with an almost perversely joyous glint in its eyes.

"Up there! Everyone. Titan!" Mathias yelled at the top of his voice.

The group looked up together.

"When did it…" Even Nikki had gone pale.

"How could we not notice?!" Klaus' teeth were clenched tight.

Jarratt lifted the barrel of the rifle. "It's dead…"

"Do not fire!" Bernhardt commanded, for some reason stopping the man.

"Boss?"

"What do you think you're doing? Hurry up and fire!" the soldier commanded, all blood gone from his face.

Moving like a cat, his footsteps utterly silent, Bernhardt closed on him. "Forgive me," he said, throwing his arms around the supple-skinned soldier.

Confusion spread across the soldier's face. "What are you…" Bernhardt unsheathed a blade from the man's waist. "You son of a…"

Before another word was uttered, Bernhardt stepped away from the soldier. In the same motion, he gracefully swung the blade upwards. As though it were a gentle caress.

That was all it took for the blood to gush from the soldier's neck.

The slashed man stared in horror. One of his hands started towards his throat, but the strength drained from his arm, and it fell limp before getting halfway. His whole body began to tip forwards. By then Bernhardt had circled to the side. Blood sprayed into the air, staining the earth, but the executioner hadn't a drop on him.

Mathias couldn't breathe. Too much was happening that he couldn't process. He'd seen a Titan. For the first time in his life, he'd seen a Titan at close quarters. Then a man had been murdered right in front him.

"Why… Why?!" his voice finally made it past his throat.

"Gunfire would have made too much noise. So I stopped him," Bernhardt replied, shrugging.

"That's not what I… That's not…"

"This is the opportunity we've been waiting for. I believe the main force has yet to notice the Titan. Why not use this window to take the horses?"

"But. To just kill…"

Mathias shuddered. *The man is a vicious outlaw.* The fact finally sank in with a visceral clarity. He fumbled around next to his thigh. His shotgun was there, slung from the leather belt. His fingers found the grip, but he couldn't summon enough strength in them to pull it free.

"Now we head for Quinta. Everyone, to work!"

On Bernhardt's cue, the rest of the outlaws snapped back to themselves, gulping, and sprang wordlessly into action.

The sound of breathing came down from overhead, unusually

slow.

Right… The Titan!

The expression on the creature's face was unchanged. It was reaching forwards now, still wearing the same unnaturally bright look. It had noticed Mathias and the others and was already getting ready to pounce.

Klaus clicked his tongue. Along with Nikki and Jarratt, he ran stumbling towards the main building.

They're going to steal the wagon?

A figure jumped out to intercept the trio.

"Quick!" The other soldier had noticed the Titan and come around the side of the building. The next moment, he realized his colleague was dead. "Wha… What happened?"

"This." Bernhardt's hand plunged down to the dead soldier's waist. He exercised his fingers, lightheartedly it seemed, as though he were just playing an instrument.

Seeing this, Jarratt and the others veered out of the way. A line shot into the air from the deceased soldier's waist. To Mathias it resembled a bolt of lightning.

But no, that wasn't it—it was an anchor, on a wire, from the Vertical Maneuvering Equipment.

A howl broke out.

The soldier, unharmed until a moment ago, held his hands over his chest. The anchor embedded in his flesh poked out from between his fingers. He staggered, crumpled forwards, and immediately began to convulse on the ground. The taut wire loosened into a lazy curve.

"There. Now you can be friends," Bernhardt said, alternating glances between the two regulars. A single wire joined them together.

The other trio was already beyond the building and out of sight. Their movements had been as uniform as a single organism's.

"No time for daydreaming, Mathias. Your precious friend awaits. You wouldn't want to be eaten in the middle of your quest." With the blood-soaked soldier still in his embrace, Bernhardt motioned his eyes upward.

Mathias spun around. The Titan had hauled itself onto the roof of the building without his even noticing. It was crawling in his direction on all fours. The expression on its face was still that of a kid who had found a toy to play with. The cow bellowed senselessly and began to back away.

"Now, for the other one."

Yet again, Bernhardt fumbled around the dead soldier's waist. A second wire shot into the sky, soaring upwards to pierce the Titan's eye, itself the size of a human head. The oversized eyeball exploded with a wet pop, and steam funneled out to obscure the cavity. The Titan padded a sluggish finger over the ruined socket and brought its hand back down to examine it.

"Excellent. Haven't lost the knack," Bernhardt sang his own

praises.

Mathias was unable to move; it was as though he'd been rooted to the spot. His heart pounded in his chest. He was soaked with sweat. But cold. He couldn't stop himself from shaking.

"Get ahold of yourself," Bernhardt admonished, quietly lowering the dead soldier to the ground. In a crouch, he spent an instant reeling in the wires he'd fired and made quick work of appropriating the Vertical Maneuvering Equipment. He got back to his feet and started towards Mathias.

"Uh…"

Bernhardt took him by the scruff of the neck and pulled.

Mathias was terrified. There was nothing he could do to resist. Bernhardt hauled him easily away.

The Titan was still moving in the corner of Mathias' vision, heaving its naked, dumpy frame over the roof of the stables.

It was large. Maybe a seven-meter-class.

The clouds of steam around its left eye were beginning to clear, and a large, round, glossy eye emerged anew from underneath. The creature's huge frame began to slide off the roof. It crashed face first into the ground.

Like the dead soldier.

The Titan cranked its arms around, pushing up a dirt-covered face. It didn't seem to be in pain. Its expression was as jubilant as before.

The muscles around its enormous shoulders tensed. It

continued towards them using only its arms, moving like a gecko on a wall.

"Not a pretty sight," panned Bernhardt. He continued to drag Mathias relentlessly, and they rounded the corner of the building. Just as the ex-soldier muttered, "Sorry to keep you waiting," one of the wagons appeared before them, overshooting five meters before it ground to a halt.

Jarratt was at the reins. Klaus was in control of the second wagon a little farther back, and Nikki was scrambling onto it.

Jarratt's eyes blinked repeatedly as he took in the sight of the Titan chasing them. "First one I've seen in a while. Gotta admit, they've got impact." Even he had tremors in his voice.

Tossing the Vertical Maneuvering Equipment then Mathias into the wagon, Bernhardt chided, "You might not weigh much, but I wouldn't say you're light as a feather."

Mathias felt a sharp jab of pain when he hit the floor, but that, too, felt like something happening in some far-off world. The wagon tilted as Bernhardt clambered on beside him.

After that, they came across Titans a total of four more times.

The first encounter was with a couple of seven-meter specimens that were distant enough not to notice them.

The second encounter was close enough for Mathias to come out in a cold sweat. They had just entered a wooded section of the road when a single five-meter-class appeared from behind one of the tall trees. It raced alongside them, reaching out, but ended up crashing head first into another one of the great trees. It fell, then simply receded behind them.

The third encounter was also with a single Titan. This one they only glimpsed beyond a ridge. At first they hadn't even recognized it as a Titan.

They crested the top of a hill to discover four Titans below them for their fourth encounter. Looking up and noticing the party at the same time, the creatures began to give chase almost as if they were racing against one another. These the humans eluded by lashing their horses.

Now they were in another forest, letting the animals rest. The sun was already low in the sky. The many-layered foliage masked the light, so the reddish glow hardly reached the ground.

"Three hours from here to Quinta?" Jarratt asked Bernhardt. They had both disembarked and were standing side by side, stretching.

Bernhardt turned toward the wagons. "They're pretty much empty. We should be a little quicker than that."

"Not too long after dark, then."

"This is really tasty, you know." Seated underneath one of the towering trees and paying no heed to the exchange, Nikki was wolfing down mouthful after mouthful of the smoked meat they'd snatched from the farmhouse earlier in the day.

Klaus was also against a tree, tending to his gun.

"There's something wrong with all of you," Mathias couldn't help accusing. "How can you act so composed? Like everything is normal?" Two soldiers had died, both slain by Bernhardt, one with a blade, the other with an anchor fired from the Vertical Maneuvering Equipment. "Those men... They hadn't done anything wrong."

"You mean the soldiers?" Bernhardt queried, adjusting the positioning of the very piece of equipment he'd appropriated from them.

"Clearly!"

"They hadn't done anything wrong, but they were unlucky."

"Specifically, the problem was that they were there," Jarratt elaborated, putting a hand on his waist and twisting to one side.

"What are you saying? You can't justify it like that. There was no need for it!"

"Hm, I wonder if that's the case." Bernhardt walked closer, stomping over fallen leaves and undergrowth. "How can you be so certain? Did you have another idea? Could you, in the heat of the moment, have offered me a better alternative? I would love for you to tell me what. Or rather, I would have loved for you to tell me. Had you done so, I might have gotten through all that without murdering anyone. Well?"

"Now that you put it that way... No, I can't offer any alternative. I might not, but it didn't need to be right then. If you'd waited just a little longer, we might have gotten away without anyone dying."

"Yeah, if we could spend days mulling it over," Nikki said, sucking on a bone from the smoked meat.

Bernhardt gave a dramatic nod. "She speaks the truth. Who is to say whether we would have had another chance? By acting immediately, I guaranteed us a means of getting away. That was why I made the decision."

"Still!"

"Sacrificing the two soldiers was simply part of that decision. You disapprove." Bernhardt arched his eyebrows. "But suppose I left them alone…"

"Now, that's reckless," Jarratt chimed in. "We couldn't have taken the wagons, and they would have called for backup. What could be worse?"

"Suppose I knocked them unconscious—which by the way requires a more advanced technique and is much harder than killing them, even for me. Anyhow, supposing I left them sprawled unconscious on the ground…"

"Chomp chomp, munch munch, same thing," Nikki completed. Her incredible appetite seemed to know no bounds; she had all but finished her hunk of smoked meat, originally the size of a pig's leg.

Bernhardt made another deep nod of his head. "Excellently put. Whichever the case, the soldiers would have ended up as Titan feed. Better to be dead, then, than to be eaten alive. It was a consideration, as well as a form of taking responsibility. They weren't just eaten, they were eaten *because of me*. Call it a ritual to make sure I was fully aware of my culpability."

"But…"

"Hypocrite," Klaus spat, his eyes still down on his firearm. "We're a shameless bunch. I don't remember us ever hiding that. You knew well enough the type of people we were when you asked for our help."

"But I never thought you were so…"

"You only saw what you wanted to."

"We are beyond the wall here," Bernhardt pointed out with a hint of sadness. "The rules of the interior no longer apply."

"Maybe you just lack the nerve." Klaus looked up, his eyes cold and sharp.

"The nerve?" To survive beyond the wall, to turn his back on the royal government, to forgo all dependence on his father, and to rely instead on his own wit and grit to help Rita.

Perhaps it was true that he lacked the nerve. Perhaps he'd been naive.

The scene from earlier replayed itself in his mind. The matter-of-fact way Bernhardt had killed the two soldiers, then fired the anchor at the Titan. The look on his face, detached somehow from the events taking place. Was that it? Was that the look of someone who had the nerve? Was that how Mathias had to be?

"Anyway, we needn't be so serious," Bernhardt said, trying

to lift the mood. "We should probably get going. I believe this should help us all get past the wall." He slapped the Vertical Maneuvering Equipment on his back. "I'm all for staging a glorious entrance, but I'll wager it'll be safer to sneak in."

"Plus, we have no idea what it's like inside," Jarratt agreed.

"Precisely. Once we're in, we can head straight for the treasure."

"You know what it'll mean if you've been lying?" Klaus clutched his gun's grip and wrapped a finger around the trigger.

"Of course."

"Our arrangement expires the moment we confirm that the horde exists. After that, you're free to go after your sweetheart or to commit suicide—whatever pleases you. We assume no responsibility for your means of escape, either."

"Meaning it's up to you to find your way back out through the wall."

Mathias responded with a resolute nod to Jarratt's clarification of Bernhardt's terms. He wanted nothing more than to part ways with these people as soon as possible.

***

Seated in a room within the district hall, Rita was mediating citizen disputes, a task to which she was hardly accustomed. This kind of work was usually reserved for the staff of the royal government, but as they had disappeared, leaving no one behind, she had no other choice.

The room was needlessly large. Warm air streamed through the open windows together with the faint afternoon sunlight.

On the other side of the desk stood two middle-aged women engaged in a shouting match. One was abnormally thin with an oversized chest and somehow brought the words "vulgar figure" to Rita's mind. The other was short and chubby, with frightfully greasy long hair. Although the two bore no resemblance to each other, apparently they were sisters. The chubby older sister fired spit into the air as she launched another offensive.

"I'm telling you, you lost all claim to ownership the moment you left town! You abandoned the house. It should be only natural that I inherit it now."

"You left first!"

"Don't be ridiculous. You should hear yourself! You just upped and left us behind, the first chance you had."

"It's not like I was leaving you!"

"But you did. Didn't spare us a single thought. Just left us stranded."

"I was thinking of you. Dad said we had to go, that's all."

"Uh huh, sure."

"It's true. I looked after him! Stayed with him all the way to the end, even had to see what I did."

"How do I know that's not just another lie? For all I know,

you could have sacrificed his life to save your own. Left him to die. Did you?"

"Why, you—"

"Ahem. Excuse me, ladies."

Having listened thus far, Rita saw that she needed to intercede. Amanda was at her side taking down everything that was being said, but that was all she would do to help; she'd been keeping her eyes down and acting as though the whole thing had nothing to do with her.

Rita cleared her throat, then spoke to the two sisters.

"Okay, let me see if I can get this straight. You, the younger sister, were living with your father. You, the older sister, had married and moved away from home. When the evacuation began, you, the younger, left Quinta with your father. Is that right so far?"

"Yes, leaving us behind," hissed the short and chubby older sister.

By "us" Rita assumed the woman was referring to herself, her husband, and their children.

The thin younger sister snapped her head around and began to argue back. "Didn't I just tell you that's not what happened? What else could we have done? Make the trip to your place? In the midst of all that chaos? Our house was a mess."

"I'm not surprised, the way you tried to grab anything remotely valuable."

"That was Dad's—"

"Please. If you could try to stay calm. During the evacuation, you and your father were attacked by Titans…"

"Yes, but I came back. Our wagon was destroyed, I lost everything. And Dad was killed!"

That was it. Their father had been attacked by a Titan. No doubt, he'd been eaten alive. While the surviving younger sister hadn't gone into the details, she must have witnessed the entire thing. A Garrison soldier had rescued her, and she'd barely made it back to Quinta with her life.

It wouldn't have been surprising if she were in shock. Instead, she was locked in a fierce battle, with her older sister who had remained in Quinta, over the ownership of those of her father's belongings that still remained at home.

Such greed. Such spirit. Rita was repelled and impressed in equal measure.

And yet it seemed the situation wasn't so clear-cut. Tears began to form in the thin younger woman's eyes, and her face crinkled. She bawled at the top of her lungs, "After what I had to go through! To be left with nothing… How, how, how could anyone just expect me to accept that?"

The woman, essentially, wanted compensation—some material benefit to give meaning to the horror and desperation she'd had to experience. Or perhaps, to fill the hole rendered in her heart. It appeared that she had been single her entire life. Having devoted herself to her father, perhaps she had never owned anything of value that she could say was truly hers.

Yet that was not the issue for the older sister. "Then maybe you shouldn't have run away. You could have let Dad go and stayed behind by yourself!"

"Do you really think I could do something like that?! Don't say you wouldn't have gone if you'd had the chance. You'd have left both of us to die!"

"What kind of trumped-up accusation is that?!"

Rita's head was pounding. She wished from the bottom of her heart to stay out of it.

What did the law say on all of this? She'd had the trainee Duccio make a search of the building, but he'd failed to turn up anything of relevance. Of course, even if he'd found something, Rita had no faith in her own ability to understand the contents.

"I'm really not made out for this," she muttered quietly to herself, and sighed.

Physical work she could handle. How easy it'd be for her if this were like suppressing a rioting mob. Her work over the last few days had been nothing of the sort. She'd been subjected to petition after petition: *There aren't enough doctors. There aren't enough teachers. You need to get the cobbles fixed on the streets.*

Yet, none of the staff she needed were around. Not only that, they seemed to have raided the vaults and storehouses of the district hall during the evacuation and taken everything with them.

Rita was bereft of means to respond to the residents' demands. She also lacked the personnel she needed to bring in more personnel or to collect taxes. The fact that Quinta's total population had fallen by more than half further limited the resources she could muster.

She was just about managing to run things with the help of the trainees and civilian volunteers. Even so, she had to admit the situation was dire. She hadn't had a wink of sleep in two days, and she probably wouldn't again that night.

"Well? What do you say? The house belongs to my husband and me. Yes?"

"Your husband? That squanderer?" the thin younger sister howled, her eyes bloodshot. "I'd rather have it all thrown away if it's going to him!"

"Well, go on then!"

It seemed to Rita that the two sisters were about to start physically wrestling. Under more peaceful circumstances, they might not have gotten into such an ugly argument. As things stood, Quinta was isolated, and the cost of necessities like water and food was skyrocketing. The older sister was, in her own way, desperate too. So much so that she couldn't even mourn her father's death.

Rita remembered then—the whole of Quinta was in crisis. While she sympathized with the women's plight, she couldn't spend all her time dealing with private matters.

"Ladies. I will now hand you my decision as the Garrison's acting commander," Rita hardened her tone a little as she addressed them. "The decision is only for the interim, until a suitable official is appointed by the royal government. Understood?"

"What?"

"If it's a fair decision, I guess."

They faced Rita—the elder first, then the younger—and fixed her with defiant stares. At least they seemed willing to listen. Perhaps the title of "acting commander" had had some effect. And maybe the blades that hung around her waist. Word of a whirlwind of a young acting commander silencing a mob a few days ago had already made its way throughout the district.

Rita took a deep breath to gather her thoughts, then opened her mouth to speak. "For now, I request that you maintain the status quo. You, the younger sister, will look after all assets left behind by your father. Their value will be calculated when my replacement arrives, so don't go and sell any of it please. Once the assets have been valued, we'll start proceedings to divide them between you two."

She was, she realized, simply passing the real decision-making on to government staff, but she had no knowledge of or experience in such affairs. It was all she could do.

"You'll assign someone to keep watch, I assume?" the elder sister cautioned straight away.

"To keep watch?"

"So she doesn't go and sell off anything."

"I'm not going to sell anything off!"

"Okay, yes," Rita promised without pause. "Soldiers will be monitoring the house. I'll make sure they aren't conspicuous, so they don't get in the way. But it's definitely a good idea to have troops around. I assume you are aware about the recent looting?" Rita asked the younger sister. "Things like that are liable to happen. The guards will be there to protect your assets rather than to make sure that you don't sell anything. Please think of it that way. Agreed?"

"If you're willing to send people out for free…well, yes, that would be great."

"Wonderful."

Needless to say, Rita didn't really intend to dispatch anyone to monitor the place. She knew all too well that she lacked the headcount for such work. But the sisters were not party to the details of the Garrison's situation, and there was no need to fill them in.

"You're happy, then, big sister?"

"Don't sound so puffed up," the older sister snorted and folded her arms over her chest.

The two women squared their shoulders and left without exchanging another glance. From behind, they did look a little alike.

Once they were fully gone from view, Rita slumped over her

desk and exhaled a long sigh.

"They were the last for today. I'm on my break," Amanda declared, sorting her sheets and getting up. She failed to offer even one word of appreciation despite Rita's obvious ordeal.

Thinking that at least she herself might, Rita said, "Thanks. Good work."

"But I'm not done. I've got patrols after this."

"Ah. Me too, I guess." Rita felt her heart sink, but she supposed it was better than being forced into more admin work.

That was depressing in its own way.

I really am not the brightest person, am I…

Amanda paced out of the room, and Duccio entered to take her place.

"Great work. Next is patrols, right? I think I'm coming with you."

"Oh, okay."

She couldn't appear lax in front of a trainee. Summoning all her remaining willpower, Rita got to her feet and straightened her back. Duccio, still a boy really, was like good cheer personified. Over the last few days he'd handled a workload not so different from Rita's, enough to leave him exhausted, but he let none of it show. Instead he volunteered to help at every opportunity. He seemed to hold Rita in some kind of reverence.

"Ma'am, I took the liberty of fixing up your Vertical Maneuvering Equipment!"

"Thanks. But remember, I'm only the acting commander. I don't have any real authority. I'm just trying to deal with things as they come in."

"You shouldn't be so modest! You're super strong!"

It was, of course, her fighting skills that he held in esteem, Rita realized, and she felt a little down again.

"Yeah. I'm okay at it," she conceded.

"Oh, and the owner at the bakery gave us some cake. It's really sweet. Loads of honey. She said we'd need it to keep up our strength, so we could guard her business properly. Let's eat them later!"

"That's an open bribe, isn't it?"

Maybe food couldn't be helped, she could tacitly permit… No, it was probably best to keep a strict regime. Corruption probably spread from such trivial exchanges.

Another sigh crept out. "Definitely not cut out for the brain work…"

"What's wrong?"

"Ah, nothing." Rita came around the desk. "We should go do the patrols."

"Yessum!"

"Then you're going to the bakery to return those cakes."

"Whaa…?" Duccio actually staggered with shock and dismay.

Thanks to him, Rita felt her heart and mind lighten a

fraction.

Looking through the window, she noted black and gray clouds overlapping in the distant sky.

***

"Rotten luck," Jarratt complained, shivering. "I hate it when it rains at night."

The party were all in long coats, their heads deep in hoods, but the unpleasant cold seeped in regardless. The rain came down hard enough to sting. The tumultuous noise made it difficult to hear their own voices without standing right next to each other.

Mathias stood squinting into the dark, his back pressed up against the towering fifty-meter wall.

"I don't know about this…"

They were at the north side of Quinta where the district wall intersected with Wall Maria itself. Towards the gate, the way was littered with the remains of wooden shanties. Charred and black, most had lost all but their skeletal supports. The group had concealed their wagons under some of the few that still retained their original form.

The rain had been falling for quite some time, but the faint tang of charcoal hung in the air. It couldn't have been long since the fires had gone out.

From place to place, the ground was marked with vast,

mortar-shaped cavities, signs of a bombardment. When Mathias had evacuated, the firing hadn't yet taken place. The shantytown being subjected to such violent shelling could only mean…

The Titans were right here.

Could Rita have survived? She was a Garrison soldier. It would have been her job to engage the Titans. She had gone through plenty of training, and it was hard to imagine that she'd gone down. Yet the Titans were overwhelmingly powerful—and, as the name suggested, overwhelmingly huge.

Mathias cast his mind back to the ones he'd encountered on his journey. The Titan that had clambered onto the roof of the stables only to slide back down hardly seemed to notice losing one of its eyes to Bernhardt's anchor. And the damage regenerated with alarming speed. Could humans really stand their own against such abominations?

They hadn't seen any near the district, for now.

"About what?" Jarratt asked.

"This rain. It's too loud. There could be a Titan nearby and we wouldn't even hear its footsteps."

"Don't assume we're all halfwits like you," Klaus scoffed.

"I'd rather not."

"Say that again?"

"It certainly is coming down." Bernhardt parted the front of his long coat, put both hands around his waist, and casually strode up to the wall. "It does seem to be easing, but I daresay haste remains the best option."

He flexed backwards and pulled the triggers on the hilts of both blades, simultaneously firing twin anchors up into the sky. The roar of the downpour muffled the sound of the wires cutting through the air. Even then, they all heard the crunch of the tips impacting the surface of the wall. The wires snapped taut, and Bernhardt's stance became that of a man on a swing with impossibly long ropes that reached up from either side.

"I'd say we're lucky," claimed Jarratt. "The rain's covering the noise we're making, too."

He was probably right. Had the night been clear, they'd have had to hide the wagons farther away. And there was always the chance of someone picking out a call or a shout even if they remained out of sight.

Bernhardt turned and crouched down. "A couple of trips should do it. Who wants to go first?"

Jarratt stepped forward. "If you wouldn't mind."

"Yup, yup, me too." Nikki approached Bernhardt and sprang up. She caught one of the wires in her right hand, fixed her right foot on the Vertical Maneuvering Equipment above Bernhardt's waistline, and pulled herself up.

Jarratt repeated more or less the same process, only more slowly and without rushing.

They appeared to be standing on Bernhardt's waist, but their weight was in fact being supported by the wires now implanted in the wall.

Bernhardt, for his part, seemed perfectly relaxed.

"To the heavens, then!"

The mustached ex-MP maneuvered the levers embedded in the hilts of the blades. Compressed gas fired, and the wires began to spool in.

The three figures began a smooth ascent.

They moved more slowly than Mathias had expected. Bernhardt had no doubt adjusted the speed of the rewind mechanism. He kicked off the wall every now and again as they rappelled up into the darkness.

"Impressive…"

"Don't get your gun wet," Klaus warned, as unfriendly as ever.

"I won't."

After a short while Bernhardt returned alone, looking again like he was sitting on a swing. "I assume you've grasped the basics?"

"Yes," Mathias answered with a firm nod. "Mind if I go first?" he made sure to ask Klaus.

Walking up to Bernhardt, Mathias took hold of one of the wires, put a foot on the equipment, and kicked off the ground to jump up. He wobbled a little but managed to keep his balance. The shotgun strapped to his thigh was a little bit in the way.

"You're wearing gloves, I take it? Wonderful. Don't hold on

too tight."

"Huh?"

"Use your head for once," Klaus muttered, putting his own foot on the Vertical Maneuvering Equipment.

"All on board? Okay, here we go."

As soon as Bernhardt said this the wire in Mathias' hands began to slide downwards, and downwards again.

"I see…"

Indeed, it would have been obvious if he'd used his head. The wire was being reeled in bit by bit, meaning his hand was moving up towards the anchor. If he tried to hold on without gloves, his skin would tear badly.

"Keep your mouth shut," advised Bernhardt. "You don't want to bite your tongue."

They ascended through the rain. They swung in arcs away from the wall each time Bernhardt kicked off. He was, Mathias realized, taking care that they didn't collide with the surface. Had it been the middle of the day, and not raining, they probably could have seen off into the far distance. It might have felt as though they were flying.

Instead, either because of the torrential rain or the way it blocked their lines of sight, Mathias had the illusion that he was plunging ever deeper into a vast expanse of water. This despite the fact that it was the other way around and they were soaring upwards.

Weird…

"And here we are. It's wet and slippery. Watch yourself."

Mathias swallowed. Right there in front of him was the very upper lip of the wall. The wind was, unsurprisingly, stronger than it had been below. Bernhardt had both feet planted on the wall, keeping them steady, but even then he couldn't fully dampen their sideways movement. Above them, Nikki was keeping vigilant watch against both stretches. Having already checked the frequency of patrols, and hidden and inaudible in the rain, the truth was that they had no reason to fear being spotted.

Jarratt lowered his huge frame and extended an arm. Mathias took hold and let himself get pulled up. His feet were on the flat surface of the wall before he could even think about the terror of falling. Just like his first time, the wall felt solid and secure and afforded a sense of stability comparable to standing on a stone floor.

Mathias turned to face Quinta. It was still early in the night. Numerous lights were visible towards the center. Didn't that mean most of the residents were alive and well?

"Phew…"

Jarratt folded his arms and gazed at the town below. "Doesn't look like they got in."

Klaus used his own strength to pull himself up. "Which was what we'd heard," he said.

"But there was always the danger of Titans getting in after the report was sent," Mathias objected.

"We didn't need to worry." Bernhardt reeled in the last stretch of wire and scrambled a little ungraciously up to join them. "We saw people on guard up here. And the gate was shut tight. Neither of which seems appropriate for a town in ruins, hmm?"

"I guess so."

"We truly are blessed!"

Bernhardt tugged the anchors free and pulled those in too. He strode across the wall and twirled around so his back faced inside. Then, in a manner that was disarmingly casual, and that left no time for anyone to intervene, he threw himself backwards into the air.

"What?!"

Immediately there was the hard crack of anchors being driven into the wall's surface. Mathias charged over to see Bernhard hanging on tightened wires, about a meter down, arms stretched out but his body securely attached to the wall.

"Who wants the tour first?"

"You shouldn't frighten us like that! I thought you'd fallen."

"Apologies."

Mathias realized Bernhardt and the others were watching him with grins on their faces. They were, all of them, of dubious moral character and jerks to boot.

He sighed and said, "I'll go first, if that's fine."

"Hoo." Bernhardt teased him with a smile. "No rush. Your

sweetheart is all cooped up inside the wall. She won't be going anywhere."

"Can we just go?"

Mathias crouched. He turned his back on Quinta and got down onto his stomach, then carefully began to lower his legs. His toes found Bernhardt's shoulder. Making sure his chest was flat on the wall, he let his legs reach even farther. Finally the soles of his feet landed on the surface of the Vertical Maneuvering Equipment. He started to transfer his weight, letting it take the strain. At the same time he groped for and found the wire, taking tight hold of it.

"Expertly done!"

"Could you just…stay quiet?"

Fortunately, Mathias' annoyance was taking precedence over his awareness of height and any fear.

They descended, Mathias and Klaus going first, followed by Jarratt and Nikki.

Bernhardt freed the anchors lodged some fifty meters up with a practiced twitch of his wrists and rapidly pulled the wires back in.

The nighttime town was quiet, partly due to the rain, and partly to the fact that half of the population had fled. The stillness was greater than Mathias had imagined, and he was beginning to doubt whether he'd needed to escape in such a hurry.

"I thought the town would be in a worse state, with people getting desperate from the isolation. From being surrounded by Titans."

"Might be a different story in the daylight." Jarratt might have been easygoing, but he was also realistic.

Initially they kept to the wall, getting closer to one of the wider passageways that radiated out from the center. Not surprisingly the road carried some traffic, and they heard the bustle of chatter and footsteps.

Even though he'd only been gone a few days, Mathias felt a burgeoning wave of nostalgia. Fuerth differed from Quinta in every possible way, from the design of its buildings to the size of the main roads and even the smells in the air.

"A moment please." Bernhardt waved his hand for everyone to stop. "Mathias, perhaps now is a good time for you to enlighten us as to where these treasures are kept."

All eyes honed in on him. It was understandable that they wanted to know the general direction, in order to make their way there efficiently. Mathias, for his part, no longer required the gang's company now that he was inside Quinta.

"Sure," he said.

"Where is it?" prompted Klaus.

"The residential district to the east. Not far from here."

"I see, closest to the interior side. Obvious when you think about it." Bernhardt put a hand to his chin, thinking about something. "Meaning it's the mansion. Your…father's." He'd gotten it in one guess.

"Yes."

"Even so, I imagine the mansion will be quite large. We'll need your help."

"You shouldn't have any trouble. Under a large tree in the northeast corner of the courtyard, there's an iron trapdoor. Open that and—"

"Nice, sounds about right," Nikki cut in.

Mathias nodded. "You should find my father's treasure inside. Okay, is that it?"

"What do you mean, 'Is that it'?" Bernhardt asked back.

"It's time for us to part ways. For good."

"Don't be silly. You sadden me, Mathias, hoping to part ways like that."

"But why not?"

"Can't be sure the treasure's even there." This came from Klaus.

Mathias gritted his teeth. "You don't trust me?"

"Well, we *are* outlaws," Nikki said without a hint of shame.

Jarratt folded his arms and nodded. "Just the way it is. Come on, we can be pals a little longer."

Right, until you confirm the treasure exists.

Mathias' eyes flicked to either side of the road. He knew the town like the back of his hand, but he still wasn't confident of

169

giving the four of them the slip. If he tried anything now he'd just end up being shot through, either by a gun, or one of those anchors.

"Okay," he agreed, bereft of alternatives.

"Good answer!" Bernhardt turned to the rest of his group. "Now that we know which way we're headed, I suggest we split up."

"Yes. Easier to work that way," Klaus assented.

"Five of us would only draw attention," remarked Jarratt.

Bernhardt nodded at them. "Would you two be kind enough to procure a wagon? We'll meet…" He launched into an accurate explanation of where the Kramer mansion was located. The outlaw and former member of the Military Police Brigade seemed to know everything. "Just keep an eye out for the largest mansion on the street. We'll go on ahead and make preparations to load everything up."

"Sure."

"Sounds good."

"Now then." Bernhardt turned again to face Mathias and Nikki. "If you two would like to accompany me. Any problems?"

"No."

"Yuck!" Nikki had her tongue sticking out from her hood and was catching raindrops.

Mathias suspected he'd never understand the way her brain worked, not in a hundred years.

"Wonderful. We'll see the two of you later."

Klaus and Jarratt responded to Bernhardt's words with shallow nods and left.

The three who remained pressed quickly on through the rain. Mathias stuck to alleys wherever he could. He knew the area well since his earliest days. It was like a backyard to him.

They passed a number of people but didn't seem to draw any attention. The long coats and hoods they wore to ward off the rain helped conceal the curious combination of mustached ex-soldier, petite thief of uncertain age, and merchant association heir.

In time they entered a district of high-reaching stone walls. Many of the buildings here had large inner courtyards that let in plenty of natural light. The characteristic meant that the walls along the street tended to be unadorned and fairly staid. The mansion Mathias lived in—had lived in—was one of them.

"We can get in through here."

He led them to the mansion's rear entrance. Nikki looked up and down the narrow side street, then up at the Kramer mansion.

"This is all your home, Mathias? It's big! Really big!"

"Hardly anyone passes this way. And it's night too, and raining, and—"

"Everyone who lived here was rich. They'd have been the first to evacuate. There won't be many left in this neighborhood."

"Exactly."

"Should anyone come by there's a good chance of them being outlaws like us. Or soldiers out to catch them," Bernhardt continued. An amused smile came to his face. "This is something I've been considering since we got here, but somebody seems to be maintaining a very high standard of law and order. I wonder if the soldiers are actually doing their jobs for a change." He swept his eyes over the other mansions in the street. "No signs of looting. Nothing to suggest an invasion of the poor. Yes, quite a miracle!"

"Really?"

Of course it was Rita whom Mathias thought of right away. Was she in some way helping to keep the peace? She had to be. She would throw herself into the task with twice the passion of anyone else.

"This is fortunate for us, too. You see, it increases the odds of the treasure we are here for being still untouched."

"True."

Mathias was conflicted. He was hoping the fortune was safe, but only so it would fall into the hands of thieves. He took a step towards the wooden door that served as the mansion's rear entrance. The surface was iron-plated, and a heavy-duty lock secured the edges. It wasn't going to be easy to break.

"How do you want to do this? Should we hop over the wall again?" Mathias asked.

"My, you are getting the hang of this! 'Should we hop over

the wall again?'" Bernhardt said, imitating Mathias' voice. "Spoken as though it were completely normal. Should we have breakfast? It's rather cold today, should we don an overcoat? Should we hop over the wall again?"

The man's tone was more mocking than friendly, and Mathias would have hit him were he not familiar with the former soldier's martial prowess.

Just barely controlling himself, Mathias asked, "So how are you going to get in?"

"Well, we do have Nikki with us. Surely you'd be interested to witness her particular expertise?"

"Her expertise?"

Nikki was already holding the lock and gazing at it in deep concentration. She let go for a moment and plunged a hand into her long coat to delve around inside. When it reappeared it was with a collection of thin metallic rods.

"Mind if I took the stage?"

She squatted again before the lock, clamping most of the rods between her lips. She pinched the remaining one between two fingers and inserted it into the lock's mechanism.

"Yep, obvious you're rich, this one's pretty clever," she remarked despite the metal in her mouth.

"Nikki…can pick locks?"

"Clearly! What else do you think she is up to? Is she cooking? Is she making music?"

Mathias could swear that when it came to annoying people, the outlaw was a genius.

"By the way, Mathias. I'm not sure I approve of a gentleman who stands by as a lady gets soaked in the rain."

It hadn't even crossed the junior Kramer's mind.

"Sorry." He hurried over, stretched himself above Nikki, and opened his coat so her hands wouldn't get wet. "Isn't it a bit dark?" he asked her.

"It's all in the sound and the feel."

Mathias took this to mean she didn't require any illumination to pick a lock.

After a while Nikki nodded, then turned her head to look at Mathias.

"Heheh."

"You got it open?"

Instead of answering she held the unhinged lock up to her face. Hardly any time had passed. Four, maybe five minutes at most.

Mathias got up with a giddy sensation. "When I get back to Fuerth I'm telling my father to change the locks."

"I could help you choose?"

"We'll be fine."

"It pays to listen to good counsel," Bernhardt scolded. He reached forwards and quickly pulled the door open.

The three of them walked through.

It wasn't far to the courtyard.

They made a straight line down a corridor with a curved ceiling. Familiar smells, of foliage and of scented wood, drifted on the air. Mathias' thoughts were pulled back to a memory…the memory of the day he and Rita first met. It felt as though only hours had passed, and yet it could have been centuries, too.

"Ah, yes, wonderful… This air of refinement! This aroma of wealth, of power, of erudition!"

Bernhardt seemed to dance as he walked. Mathias ignored him and headed towards the corner of the courtyard. Treading over the muddy surface, he continued until he reached the foot of the tree.

"This is it."

"Where?" Nikki was looking this way and that.

"Let me just open it."

Mathias kicked with his shoes to clear away the dirt, exposing the iron plate underneath. He crouched and, heedless of getting wet, ran his fingers through the handle. The metal was cold through his gloves. He tensed and heaved upwards with all of his might.

"Ooh, cool," Nikki offered the vaguest of impressions.

When the plate was partway open, Mathias held it still. This was to stop the rain from flooding into the underground room. Bernhardt stepped up and peered inside.

"Anything to suggest it's been looted?"

"No," Mathias informed him. "We didn't see any footprints. And why cover it with dirt, if it was empty?"

"Good points. I suppose it's about the size of an ordinary household's bedroom?"

Mathias' thoughts went to the bedrooms in Rita's home. He'd never used them, but he'd been inside. "Yes. Pretty much."

"I think I'll take a look, then."

"Please."

"No reason for us all to go in." Bernhardt cast his eyes toward the cloisters that surrounded the courtyard. "Would you be kind enough to wait for a bit? Both of you. You won't get wet if you stand under there."

"Fine. What do you want to do about the lid?"

"I assume you can open it from the inside? I know I wouldn't make one that didn't."

"It does, yes."

"Then feel free to close it. It wouldn't do for the treasures to get wet."

"What about lighting?"

"I wouldn't be so unprepared!" Bernhardt pulled open his coat to produce a lantern from somewhere underneath.

Impressive...

Mathias nodded and stepped to one side, raising the iron lid until it was vertical.

Bernhardt proceeded down without hesitation. From below came the sound of a flint being struck, and pale light streamed out immediately.

"Good. No problems with airflow," his voice sounded.

"I'm closing the lid." Reversing the steps, Mathias shut the trapdoor.

He noticed that Nikki had moved to the cloisters. And that she held her rifle in her hands. She didn't seem to be aiming at anything, but only moments earlier, the weapon had hung from her shoulder on a leather belt inside her coat so it wouldn't get wet.

"Why…" Mathias began to ask, but the answer flashed into his mind.

She was ready to act if Mathias didn't fulfill his end of the bargain—if the concealed riches failed to materialize, or if he tried to run.

Having worked through that much, Mathias hit upon the horrific truth.

Bernhardt had no reason not to dispose of him right there, whether or not the hidden treasure existed. If anything, it would behoove the man to get rid of Mathias. If the artworks were still there—and Mathias had good reason to believe they were—killing him would remove the only person in the world who could identify the thieves. It significantly lowered the chances of the Military Police Brigade coming after them.

Attack on Titan

Not good. Not. Good.

Mathias' fingers traced down the inside of his long coat and reached his thigh. Freeing the shotgun from its clasp, he brought his other hand over to hold it crossways over his stomach.

The time might come for him to actually need it.

Nikki had the muzzle of her rifle pointed towards the ground; she wouldn't be able to fire right away. She was pressing her free hand into the windows and doors lining the cloisters, keeping Mathias in the corner of her eye as she surveyed inside. The first floor contained the kitchen, the dining room, and the servants' quarters, so few of the doors were locked.

Mathias approached the cloisters as though everything were normal. He wanted to keep his distance, but Nikki might grow suspicious if he lingered in the rain. He crossed over the earth in wet shoes.

He reached the stone-slab flooring of the cloisters.

"Stop right there!"

The voice wasn't his. Nor was it Nikki's. It had emanated from the corridor to the rear entrance that they had passed through.

Mathias' head snapped up.

A soldier with close-cropped hair had his rifle raised. He looked young enough to still be a boy, younger than Mathias. And yet, he wore the uniform of a Garrison soldier. Perhaps he was just baby-faced.

The boy's whole body was trembling. Mathias somehow

sensed this even though they were over five meters apart.

The boy could only be seeing the scene as an encounter with some scoundrels who were robbing a wealthy family. How could he know that that was only half of the truth?

Mathias brought his shotgun up on reflex alone. The movement parted the front of his coat.

The weapon in his hands abruptly exploded.

What the…

No, he'd managed to pull the trigger by mistake. There was a sound up ahead like an egg cracking.

He heard Nikki gulping nearby.

Mathias looked up.

The boy from before was beginning to fall backwards. There was something wrong with his face.

Something had changed.

Something was missing.

Don't tell me…

Mathias finally realized what. The right side of the boy's head was gone, blown away.

Each passing second felt stretched out.

"Duccio?!"

It was a female voice that screamed this time.

A familiar voice. One that overflowed with vitality.

Except now, it was tinged with astonishment and despair.

In its wake a woman wearing the Garrison's uniform came

running into view. The voice had to be hers. A comrade or such of the boy whose head was half-gone.

A howl caught in her throat when she saw the boy in mid-fall. She raced over, reaching with her arms, but arrived a moment too late. The boy threw out his arms and legs on the stone-slab floor.

The insides of his head splattered out, plastering the woman's legs and shoes.

She lifted her head.

Mathias had already guessed it. Of course, it had to be.

"Rita…"

They'd been reunited.

Her mouth was opening and closing as she gasped for air. "Why…"

A shot rang out next to Mathias. Fireworks sparked off the wall beside Rita. It took a moment for Mathias to work out what had happened. Nikki had fired her rifle.

"For now," Nikki said, casual. She took Mathias by the scuff of his neck and dragged him with a strength that seemed to belie her build. All the while she kept firing rounds from her rifle with one hand, transforming the wall where Rita had been into a pockmarked mess. "Happens a lot," she said, her voice perfectly absent of strain. The incredible force with which she hauled Mathias remained unchanged.

Why do I always let these people drag me around? Mathias reflected as though it concerned someone else.

Nikki was moving with brisk steps and was almost on the door that led to the corner room. She hurled her rifle down, opened the door, and threw Mathias in before following in behind him. It was dark, except for a square of pale light shining through the wall—a window.

Nikki tore the shotgun out of Mathias' hands. She aimed the muzzle at the window and fired. Mathias was deafened by the thunderous report as the shutters exploded outwards from the middle.

The scene from moments ago replayed in his thoughts. The boy's head, blown apart. Rita showing up, her eyes stretching wide in distress and horror. Her hand reaching for the body as it collapsed. Her eyes unbelieving as they turned towards Mathias. Rita actually asking him: "Why?" He hadn't known how to respond.

Rita...

His hearing was slowly returning.

"Yup, yup. First we get out."

Nikki lobbed the shotgun to one side and used both hands to grab Mathias by his clothes. She pulled him forwards, employing the momentum to catapult him into the wreckage of the shutters.

There was an impact, then a sudden jolt of pain. The sense of being airborne came next.

Mathias sailed into a narrow street together with the fragments of the shutters...and started to fall. Unable to bring himself around, he crashed down into the hard cobbled surface.

He was set upon by the rain and cold.

A grimy puddle of water splashed into his face. When he looked he saw that Nikki had landed soundlessly next to him. She took his collar and pulled him to his feet.

A part of his brain realized he was in a side street. Dark mansion walls towered on either side. It felt claustrophobic, as though they were bearing in on him. The sky was narrow and distant, but the rain came as though it was being tipped from a pot.

The same scene continued to play itself over and over. The boy soldier's face, blown apart. Rita coming into view, running up to the boy. The turmoil of emotion in her eyes…

I'll need to explain.

But how? What could he say that would make her understand? How could he possibly justify what he'd done?

"Hmm, that way?"

Nikki began to walk, dragging Mathias behind her. She hadn't lost her composure. She was acting exactly as she usually did, humming an out-of-tune melody to herself, stroking the wall for no discernible reason. There didn't seem to be any logic or continuity to anything she did.

Except—maybe that wasn't true. As far as their survival was concerned, her actions hadn't once strayed from the mark.

Nikki came to a stop and poked her head around the side of the building. She was checking the situation on the road.

"Ah, that's what I call good timing." She observed a while longer, then stepped forward without ceremony. Mathias was pulled into the road with her.

A wagon approached. One man was driving it, while another stood in the uncovered cart. Nikki strolled down the street with no apparent concern, her arm slung around Mathias' shoulder.

They were, by now, completely soaked, and Mathias' hair hung wetly over his forehead.

The wagon started to slow, eventually coming to a full stop beside them.

"Something wrong?" the driver said from under his hood. The voice belonged to Klaus.

"I think Bernhardt got detention," Nikki shared, springing onto the wagon.

"Damn it," Klaus swore.

The man on the cart—judging by his size, Jarratt—extended two bulky arms towards the road.

"It happens, I suppose," the old man said. Taking hold of Mathias on both sides, he hoisted him lightly into the air and set him roughly down by his side. "We'll need to get out of here, for now."

"Agreed."

Without a pause Klaus whipped the horse.

The wagon began to move, and the vibration rocked Mathias up and down. His joints ached from his earlier fall.

The farther they got from his childhood home, the more he felt like throwing up.

"Rita…"

Unable to bear it, Mathias leaned over the lip of the wagon and actually vomited a little.

The rain washed the juices from the street.

Things weren't right.

They weren't supposed to be this way.

CONTINUED IN PART 2

The Harsh Mistress of the City

of

the City

COMMENTARY

On Giggle Akiguchi, Author and Sworn Friend

Under the nom de plume Giggle Akiguchi, this book's writer, Ryo Kawakami, won the special jury award for the 10th Fantasia Novel Award. He's a veteran who made his debut in 2000 with the winner, *Parallel Bio*.

He is renowned for his powerful action sequences and group dramas where multiple characters stand tall.

He also wears another hat as a celebrated game designer. Without the tenacity and aptitude for probing, disassembling, and reconstructing the matter at hand whatever it may be, you can't establish yourself as a game designer. For novelizations, where you're entrusted with someone else's work, that tenacity and aptitude become extremely valuable.

This book, *Attack on Titan: The Harsh Mistress of the City: Part 1*, is indeed a masterpiece worthy of the seasoned novelist and brilliant game designer Giggle Akiguchi.

The depictions of numerous fascinating characters, the dashing action. By harmonizing these with an almost obsessive inquiry into the world of *Attack on Titan*, the book crystallizes into a gemstone of a piece.

The compiling mysteries, and Mathias' and Rita's wishes. Purpose, heart. The far reaches of the tale to which they beckon are still beyond sight. Start preparing for the impact, now. It's bound to be a blissful experience.

Kiyomune Miwa
Attack on Titan Settings Contributor

POISON

Quinta, isolated by

Rita wishes to

GALLOWS

while Mathias

Their hearts

EXPLODED

Attack on Titan

COMING

the Titans' incursion.

RULER

safeguard order,

must rein her in.

SENSELESS

cruelly at odds.

TITAN

The Harsh Mistress of the City
Part 2

VERY SOON!!

HUNGRY FOR MORE

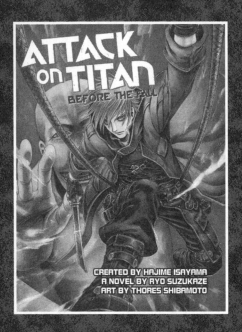

Attack on Titan Before the Fall

Before the fall, and before the trials of "the Titan's son" Kuklo, a young smith by the name of Angel Aaltonen grapples with the giants as only a craftsman can in this first official novelization.

"At one point, while prodding and cutting up a Titan in an attempt to uncover a weak point—any weakness at all that might provide a shred of hope—Angel finds himself conflicted. 'Why does he have to look so human? Look more like a monster, you monster...' he pleads. That's why I dig *Attack on Titan*." —*Otaku USA*

BOTH VOLUMES

ATTACK ON TITAN?

Attack on Titan Kuklo Unbound

Swallowed and regurgitated as an infant by a Titan, an orphan seeks to find and prove himself in this official prequel novel to the smash hit comics series. A stand-alone work (whose ongoing manga adaptation is available stateside from Kodansha Comics as *Attack on Titan: Before the Fall*), *Kuklo Unbound* offers a rare window into the era preceding the destruction of Wall Maria and features must-know bits like the rebirth of the Survey Corps and rumors of a rogue settlement beyond humanity's cage.

AVAILABLE NOW!